ELEGY
BOOK ONE OF THE ARBITER CODEX

BY
CHRISTOPHER KELLEN

Original Digital Publication Date: July 2011

1st Print Edition: March 2012
Eisengoth Independent Books

Original Cover Artwork by
Zoe Cannon &
Kylen Wiggin

Twitter:
@Eisengoth

Website:
http://www.christopherkellen.com

Thanks go to Zoe, Roberta, Elene and Kayla for all of their thoughtful input that really made this story come together. To Dave K. whose early enthusiasm for my work was a great inspiration to keep going.

Last but not least to Michael, whose patient advice and masterful insight I have only just begun to know, but which I expect to take me much farther than I could have gone on my own.

Praise for Elegy

The Arbiter Codex series has definitely catapulted to the top of my must read list whenever a new installment is released.

— Amazon.com User Review

A truly fantastic read! I enjoyed every minute of it. Christopher has built a very intriguing and complex world that captivates the reader from the very moment they begin reading his book. The action starts at the very beginning and is consistent throughout the entire story. I recommend this sword and sorcery fantasy to all those who enjoy reading fantasy books.

— Lissette, Simplistik.org Book Review

"As a publisher for fantasy, I am very critical about what I read in my spare time and have found many books that I cannot read past page 20 (or even 10 for that matter). Different with this one. It kept me away from my work far too often and for that, I thank Kellen sincerely."

— Goodreads.com User Review

TABLE OF CONTENTS

BONUS STORY:
ON THE LAST DAY OF LIGHT

AFTERWORD
ABOUT THE AUTHOR
MORE BY CHRISTOPHER KELLEN

I
THE MAUSOLEUM

He knew that he was being followed.

The pale moon hung heavily in the sky as the night wore on, casting everything in long grey shadows. Winter had come to the outlands; no snow yet lay on the ground, but the leaves had all fallen from the trees, and the ground was cracked from the freezing temperatures that crept across the land at night. There was no color on a night like this, no colors on the trees with the leaves fallen, and all else washed away in the light of the Deadmoon.

Mist formed from each breath before him as the great destrier beneath him plodded onward towards their destination. The horse seemed nervous, and his horse was rarely ever nervous. The city of Calessa still lay at least a league away, and they were already in danger.

It seemed that he was always in danger.

"Come, Tyral." He urged the horse onward in a low tone, and despite the cold, the great beast managed to pick up its pace.

He rode onward through the starkly bare trees, casting his eyes about him at all times, expecting that any moment they might attack from the shadows. Traveling at night was a dangerous pastime, and most of those who tried it would fall prey to the horrific creatures that prowled the outlands in the moonlight.

At last, the great stone walls of Calessa hove into view. He had found refuge at last, a savior from the bitter cold. He could see smoke curling lazily upward from chimneys and lights, though they were few indeed, this close to dawn.

The walls seemed to grow to an immense height as he approached them. It had escaped him just how high the walls of the city were, built of thick and hardened stone to protect against the horrors that lay just outside them. The dusty road upon which he traveled led straight to the vast wooden gates that admitted visitors into the city.

As they approached the gate, he drew the horse to a stop. "By authority of the Arbiters, I command you to open the gate and admit me to your city!" he called up towards the top of the walls.

There was no answer.

There came from the edge of the barren forest through which he had passed a low, throaty growl. He turned the horse around to see three beasts lingering near the edge of the forest. Twisted mockeries of the creatures they had once been, they stood almost two feet tall at the shoulder. Though they were vaguely canine, no dog would claim them as kin now. Huge teeth, too large for their heads, were bared in anticipation, and their massive claws stood out from huge, oversized paws. In the dark, he could see their eyes glowing a dull, angry red, the color of the corrupted manna that lent them their twisted shape. They eyed him hungrily but did not yet approach, for they knew that what lay on the other side of their gates was their death for certain.

A lonely traveler, alone outside the gates of the city… that was almost a certain victory for the hungry creatures.

"Fel dogs," the traveler spat under his breath. He looked sharply up once more at the wall. "Open the gods-damned gates, I say!"

Still there was no response from the impassive stone.

"Damn," he cursed viciously. "Nothing for it, then."

With a smooth motion he swung his leg over the back of the horse and dismounted. The destrier snorted and stepped nervously sideways once the rider had disengaged.

He reached to his back and pulled free the long, straight blade that hung lightly on his baldric. The crystalline blade came free with a low rasping noise, and the area flooded with a blue glow, the pure manna flowing through the blade and lending him strength. He gripped the blade's handle tightly in both hands, and gave a quick nod toward the horse, who took a few more steps away.

The walls would protect the city.

Seeing that their prey had suddenly decreased in size, the fel dogs' confidence increased tenfold. The blue light from the manna blade made them uneasy, but though the corrupted life force had given them size and strength, it had not given them a worthy intelligence.

They charged.

The traveler braced himself against the charge. He waited; the beasts were closing rapidly, and he kept his eyes trained on the foremost, the largest. That one would fall first, and the others would follow swiftly.

The beast leapt at him, baring those monstrous teeth, a mouth large enough to swallow his entire head in one bite. The claws glistened in the moonlight, the combination of blue and red light bathing both in violet.

He made one swift motion, a half-turn that brought him below the outstretched claws, and then his arms went up, the crystalline blade cutting a long stroke along the beast's underbelly. It was not the killing stroke he had hoped for, but as the beast passed by him it let out an unearthly shriek.

It landed on the ground a few feet away, dripping luminescent fluid that pooled on the ground beneath it. As the traveler turned to meet the eyes of the beast, it let out a low, rumbling growl. The voices of the others joined it and the noise rose to a howl, a cacophony that threatened to deafen him.

"Beast!" the traveler shouted, rushing forward with a downward stroke intended to cleave the creature's head from its shoulders.

The fel dog leapt aside and came back immediately, its claws raking the air as the man took a step backward, out of its reach. He sensed that the others were circling around behind him, waiting for a moment when he was not watching them, so that they could bring him down as a pack.

He spun about, releasing one hand off the grip of his sword. Blue fire began to collect around his newly freed hand, and he let out a cry as the manna fire leapt from his thickly gloved hand at the two fel beasts. One managed to get out of its way, but the fire caught the other directly in the abdomen. The creature let out an echoing yip as the fire struck it, and then as though it had a malevolent intelligence all its own, the fire began to devour it.

Its yip turned into a horrible howl of pain as the blue flames devoured its flesh, reducing it within seconds to nothing but a red glow that quickly absorbed into the earth, the corrupted manna returning to the land for purification.

"One down," he said with a small smile.

The other two were now circling warily in the other direction. He came about to face them, one wounded and still dripping viscous fluid – it could not be called blood, for it had ceased to flow long ago – the other still hale but its confidence shaken by the sudden loss of its companion.

He once again set his stance with both hands on the blade, and waited.

The wounded one, the alpha, was the first to charge. The wound it had taken had enraged it now, and the dull red fire in its eyes had brightened in fury. Its charge was surefooted and sound, but the wound had slowed it. It feinted and snapped its teeth to the left, but he had anticipated its deception. When it moved back to make its true attack, he sank the crystalline blade deep into the beast's neck. It let out a strangled cry and the thick fluid poured forth from the new wound.

He twisted the blade sharply, and that was the end of the beast. It dropped to the ground, and blue fire crept down the crystalline blade of its own volition, the pure manna seeking to purify the corruption, to cleanse it of its evil. Soon, the blue flames were licking at the corpse, and as they caught they clung to the fur, to the flesh, and reduced it in a flash to the same retreating red glow.

As he pulled the blade free, he turned to face the last of the fel dogs. He stared at it defiantly, daring it to attack him as well, to meet the same fate as its two companions. It stared back, meeting his eyes for a moment. Though the manna had twisted its form and robbed it of many an instinct, self-preservation was still strong in its brain. The prey had outwitted it, and though pride was badly damaged, the desire to continue existing overrode the rage to attack.

It turned tail and fled, back into the frozen forest.

None of the luminescent fluid from the slain beast remained on the blade. It had been consumed by the manna within the sword. He positioned it carefully and slid it back home into the scabbard on his baldric, and the blue glow vanished as it clicked home. He flashed the horse a smile, and the beast rolled its eyes and huffed a sigh.

The great gate cracked open behind him. He turned to face it, and saw the wooden barrier beginning to part. From within, a soldier walked forward, his polished steel armor gleaming in the moonlight.

"That was quite the display," the soldier said amicably.

"It won't soon be returning," the traveler said, staring off into the forest after the beast. "Not until it gathers its pack."

"You're an Arbiter?" the soldier asked, after looking him up and down. "You won't be much liked in Calessa. There's plenty of evil here… if you go looking for it, you'll find it."

"I am an Arbiter, not an Inquisitor," he responded. "I do not search for the evil of men. I have no care for those who break the laws of men. I have come to Calessa because the manna has drawn me here.

"Look around at the forest. The life force has become corrupted, your trees die, the ground is frozen and yet there is no snow. Great beasts roam the forests. I would be surprised if any trade caravans have made it here in months. The manna has become corrupted here, and I am to set it right." He gestured widely with his hand, indicating the land about them as he spoke.

"How do you intend to do that?" the soldier asked.

The Arbiter merely smiled at the man. His eyes took on a fervent gaze, and his irises began to glow softly with the blue light of the manna.

The soldier quickly became uncomfortable. "As I said,

you won't be much liked here in Calessa, but since you drove off those fel dogs, I'll allow you inside. Please declare your name and occupation."

"My name is D'Arden Tal," the traveler said. "I am an Arbiter."

**

The city was quiet in the dark hours of the morning, those few last moments before the first rays of light began to break the horizon. Only a few torches burned outside buildings; most had been extinguished. The square inside the gate he had entered would have normally been crowded with traders and shoppers, he guessed, and it was almost strange and intimate to see the streets so devoid of life.

Across the way he spied a building which was still brightly lit, even in these dark hours. There were lanterns blazing on a small sign near the street that pointed down a small foot path to the building that read 'TAVERN'.

He nodded to himself. Not only were rest and sustenance important, but he also needed a base of operations – somewhere to begin building his investigation.

Giving the horse a sharp tug on its reins, he began to walk towards the low-set building. The roof slanted slightly downward as it traveled from right to left, and the wooden slats looked to be worn, but not worn out. There was a fair-sized stable that was barely visible around the right-hand edges of the main hall.

There would be food and lodging for both of them tonight.

As he approached the sign, a boy stepped out from behind it. D'Arden was momentarily shocked to see such a young lad out so late – or, truly, up so early – but the boy offered out a friendly hand to take the horse's reins.

"Will you be staying with us tonight, master?" the boy asked.

"Indeed I will," D'Arden said after a moment. He handed the boy the reins with one hand, and with the other, pressed a thick silver coin into the boy's other hand. The lad took a quick glimpse at it, grinned… and then the coin was gone, and the boy was leading the great beast away to the stables where it would be happily brushed and given all the grain it could eat for the day.

He started up the short footpath to the low-lying building and pushed the door open when he reached it. Warm light spilled forth from the threshold, but only a few sounds of life came from within. He stepped quickly inside and closed the door behind him to keep the cold at bay.

All of the tables inside, which in the evening would have been filled with loud, raucous laughter and the banging of glasses and shouting, were silent. There were only a few still awake: one man in the corner near the merrily blazing fireplace who appeared to be nursing a bottle of some kind, and another sitting at a table all the way across the room from the door, his head bowed and appearing to sleep without having made it to his chamber for the night.

"Mornin', master," came a voice from the counter. A slender, wiry man with thick hair and small, squinted eyes looked over at him from where he stood, polishing a glass with an old rag.

D'Arden favored him with a slow nod. "Good

morning."

"Travelin' all night, have you been?"

"Indeed I have."

The publican looked him over slowly, tilting his head with interest. "How'd you get them guards to let you in before dawn?"

D'Arden fixed one manna-blue eye on the man. "There were beasts outside. Fel dogs. I killed them."

The other man nodded appreciatively, bobbing his head a little too far each time. "That would do it, all right. They always looking for another sword to keep the city safe."

"Perhaps," D'Arden said.

"Good then." The publican nodded once more before turning back to the alcohol behind the bar. "Looking for a drink this early morning, or just some rest?"

"Neither, actually." D'Arden stepped more fully into the room and crossed it with a few quick strides to stand next to the counter. The tavern-keeper seemed startled by his sudden approach, but made little external movement. "I do need to rent a room from you, but then I will be gone for a short time. Tell me, where is this city's closest font?"

The publican's eyes stretched wide, wider than D'Arden would have thought imaginable. "Why would you want to know a thing like that? Those things is dangerous, you know. We won't have any sorcerers staying at my house!"

D'Arden shook his head. "Worry not. I am no sorcerer. They are unpredictable and dangerous, working the manna to their own ends, for personal gain and power."

15

The other man stared at him with such shock in recognition that D'Arden almost smiled broadly. "Y...you are..." the man stammered.

"Correct," D'Arden said, barely managing to contain that same smile.

"We've not seen one of your kind about here in five years! My house is your house, master Arbiter! P... please do not think that my..."

D'Arden held up a soothing hand. "Worry not. Your conviction was so strong about having no sorcerers under your roof that it nearly echoed in the life-force around you. You and your family are safe."

"Th...thank you, master Arbiter!" the publican's relief was evident, as was the stench of the sweat that had suddenly come over the man in his nervousness. He leaned in conspiratorially, and it was all D'Arden could do to keep from choking on the man's smell. "The font's few blocks down. We can't control where they come up, but the soldiers always build them stone chapels around 'em that's locked away from outsiders. If you've got a friend in the garrison, that'll be your ticket inside."

"And the room?"

"For you, master Arbiter, minimal charge. Two silver a week."

D'Arden nodded. "And a third for the good care of my horse."

"Of course, of course," the publican said, reaching under the counter to pull free one of the keys from the rack, and then handing it to the Arbiter. "It be the largest room I have left available tonight."

"It will suffice," D'Arden said, tucking the key into one of the pockets of his great black cloak. "For now, I

16

must go and find the font."

"Be wary, master Arbiter," the tavern-keeper said. "Terrible things walk the streets of Calessa these days. It seem nowhere is safe."

Without even making a movement toward the stairs that would take him to his room, D'Arden walked swiftly back to the door to the bitterly cold outside and stepped through it, careful not to let too much of the inviting heat creep out.

The sky was beginning to show its first signs of light, and D'Arden knew that if he was going to make his way inside the font chapel, he would have to do so before too many were awake. Breaking into the chapel was a possibility, but he quickly decided against that – there was too much at stake here, and alerting the townsfolk to the possibility of a rogue sorcerer was too dangerous.

He would have to hope that the guard who had let him in at the gate would be amenable enough to allowing him to access the font.

A few long strides carried him back over to the gate, which was once again closed and locked, barring entry from the outside world. A few of the soldiers approached cautiously, and D'Arden quickly recognized the man who had let him inside the city.

"Leaving again so soon are ye, master Arbiter?" the soldier asked.

D'Arden shook his head. "No. I need to get inside the font chapel."

"Nobody goes in there," the soldier said. "Sorry, captain's orders."

"It's important," D'Arden insisted. "I need to read the manna here, to determine what is causing the corruption that you see all around you. Can you even grow plants in this city, with the way it is right now? How long has it been since the ground has thawed?"

The soldier considered for a moment, then shook his head. "I'm sorry, master Arbiter. I can't make that decision. The captain would skin me alive if he found out. You'll have to get his leave to enter the chapel."

"Very well," D'Arden said. "Where can I find this captain of yours?"

"He takes reports from all of the night shifts at the garrison," the soldier said, pointing down one of the streets. "You'll find the garrison at the end of that road. He's up all night, like us. It's the night that's the most dangerous around here. Nothing happens during the day except people freezin' to their deaths in alleys."

Without another word, D'Arden turned on one heel and walked away from the soldier. "Useless," he muttered under his breath. "This captain must run a tighter ship than I'm used to."

Along the street, all of the buildings were dark. The gate he'd come in by was obviously the trader's gate, as all of them were storefronts of some kind. Food, trinkets, metal; this place would be busier than a honeycomb during the day. The lodging he'd chosen would be perfect to observe the populace for suspicious activity.

The garrison sat at the end of this dead-end street. There were alleys that connected it to other streets, but directly at the end of this one was a small flare of the cobblestones and a large sign posted at the center, just in front of the larger, still-lit building identifying this as the soldiers' barracks. D'Arden surmised that this must be the area of most danger; either that, or this area had not always been the trade quarter, and the soldiers hadn't moved once the merchants started coming here in more force.

The garrison door was closed, but as he tested the handle, he found that it was not locked. As he swung open the heavy wooden portal, two soldiers emerged from hallways on the left and right to watch him carefully as he stepped inside and closed the door behind him.

"State your business," one of the soldiers said.

"My name is D'Arden Tal. I am an Arbiter, here on business. I need to speak with your captain of the guard." The soldiers wore a combination of red and silver. He could see it now, in the warm light of the interior. Outside, under the light of the Deadmoon, everything looked grey. The symbol of Calessa, the great circle with two cross-strokes bisected by a sword, was displayed proudly on the chest of each man, emblazoned in silver on the background of the red tabard. Neither wore the thick half-helmets that the soldiers outside did, but it was also several degrees warmer within than without.

The soldier on his right was tall, had a thick shock of brown hair and was clearly the dominant presence in the room; the soldier on his left was shorter, thinner and generally less imposing. It surprised him then that it was the shorter soldier who turned sharply on his heel and barked out, "Follow me. I will take you to the Captain."

Rapidly overcoming his surprise, D'Arden nodded and fell in line with the other soldier.

As they opened a door to one of the back rooms, a man looked up from behind a desk, looking tired and weary. His hair was short and curled, and he wore grizzled, graying stubble that looked as though it hadn't been trimmed in days. There were thick lines around his eyes, and they were set deep as though the man hadn't slept in a fortnight.

"Yes, what is it, Ralda?" the elder man asked, setting down his quill.

"An Arbiter has come to see you, captain," the shorter soldier, who had now been identified as Ralda, said sharply.

A look of mild surprise came over the captain's face. "Indeed? Well, send him in then. There is no reason to keep an Arbiter waiting."

Ralda stepped aside to allow D'Arden access to the room. With a curt nod, D'Arden stepped past him and into what was obviously the captain's war room. There were maps of the city strewn across every wall, every surface. On one there was a map with several small figurines which D'Arden quickly deduced represented each patrol that was on guard that night and where they were positioned. He quickly committed the information to memory; it could be useful if things went sour here.

"It has been many years since an Arbiter has come to our city," the Captain said. He gestured to a chair that waited on the close side of the desk. "Please, sit. My name is Captain Aldur Mor."

D'Arden hesitated a moment, and then took the proffered seat, being careful not to trap the blade that was on his back so that it could not be drawn in case of an emergency. "I realize that my kind is not particularly welcome here, Captain."

Captain Mor smiled. "Indeed, that is true. The last of your kind that came to Calessa… well, let's simply say it wasn't a pleasant situation. Several of my men died, and approximately a hundred citizens were slaughtered by that crystal sword that you carry. The bastard never left here."

D'Arden arched an eyebrow. "Indeed?"

"We couldn't kill him, if that's what you're asking," Captain Mor said, his voice turning slightly bitter. "Our arrows, our swords just fell off of him. He was drawing power from the font near Central Square, and all the while he was turning bright red. Not a flush in his cheeks, mind you, but a real, malevolent glow to him. When he was done clearing out the old fort, he descended into the catacombs below it and never came out."

The Arbiter nodded. "The corruption would have torn him apart before long. You can rest assured of that, Captain."

"Well then." Mor paused a moment, then looked back up at D'Arden. "How can I serve you? One evil man does not stain the good name of the Arbiters of the world, and I would do all I can to assist your endeavors."

"I believe this next question may be a bit awkward, Captain, in light of the tale you have told to me," D'Arden said with slight hesitation. "I need access to the font chapel nearby, so that I may read the manna. I believe…" he lowered his tone considerably so that it was just above a whisper, "…that there may be a demon present in your city."

"A true demon?" the Captain's face went white. "A fel beast you mean, surely."

D'Arden shook his head. "Have you been outside the walls of your fair city, Captain Mor? No plants grow outside. The trees have lost their leaves, and where it should be early spring, I find only a frozen ground with no snow. The ground is cracked and raw, fel beasts hunt through the dead forest. Only one being could have corrupted the manna in such a way. You have a true demon on your hands."

"There has never been a true demon in Calessa!" Mor said, his voice sounding thickly of despair. "We have always stood vigilant against the fel, never allowing any such beast to enter!"

"This is the very task for which we exist, Captain. My order was given birth to by the last King Damedeys in the last Age, not to hunt and extinguish the evils of men, but to combat the great evils that lurk in the darkness, that corrupt our land and our people by destroying the life-force, the manna."

"This is very troubling indeed, if what you say is true." Mor leaned back in his chair and brought one hand up to his chin. "But… I cannot simply give you access to the font chapel. The people are too afraid. They would riot if they knew that there was once again an Arbiter walking among us, and I do not have the manpower to control a riot."

"You will have no citizens left to protect if you allow this demon to grow to its full power," D'Arden said with only a slight chime of warning in his voice.

"I understand," Mor said with a sigh. "Listen. There is a crypt standing in a graveyard outside the city. It is less than a furlong from the walls. Within there some have heard horrific sounds, and I fear that there may be fel beasts raising the dead inside. Will you go there and cleanse the crypt? There is a font chapel within the graveyard itself, and while it may not give you enough knowledge of the city, it should be enough power for you to draw on to complete your task."

"And if I cleanse the crypt, you will allow me access to the chapels within the walls of your city?"

The captain nodded.

"Very well then," D'Arden said with a nod. "I will cleanse your graveyard."

"Excellent," Mor said, standing. D'Arden did the same. "When can you begin?"

The Arbiter gritted his teeth. "I will begin immediately."

**

He'd left his horse happily munching away in the stable. The crypt lay only a short way out of town, and there was no point in dragging the great beast into a graveyard full of the wakened dead.

Dawn had come as he made his way to the crypt, creeping over the horizon with its tendrils of light but bringing no warmth to the frozen landscape. If the Deadmoon had caused the land to look sparse and unfriendly in the darkness of the night, the sun's light did little to help it. Dead trees stood like stark skeletons against the slowly lightening sky, with no hint of leaves remaining in their branches. The stench of decay was strong, and it was easy to tell when he passed by the trees that they were rotting from the core. The corruption here was strong, and it would take a long time for the region to recover once the evil here was stamped out completely.

Men are ridiculous, he mused. *If that idiot captain had simply allowed me to access the font, I could have been on the trail of the demon by now. If I'd slain the demon, the graveyard would have ceased to be a problem.*

There was a low, cold mist hanging over the graveyard as he approached. The stones stood stiffly from the ground, most unmarked. Only the richest could buy a grave alone, and those were clearly separated in a gated area a few hundred feet from the common graves. The rising sun cast long shadows across the mounds and gave the entire scene a reddish cast.

He stopped and listened for a moment. There were no sounds here. No birds sat in the dead trees – they would have fled long ago. The fel beasts would be hiding, keeping out of the sunlight that was deadly to them.

Across the low rising field was a small stone chapel, and beside it sat a massive mausoleum. He fixed his eyes on the chapel and began striding toward it.

When he reached the great wooden door, he noticed that it had fallen slightly ajar. The hinges were rusted and failing. He shook his head disdainfully. The power contained inside each and every one of these chapels was both precious and extremely dangerous. It was likely that the demon had something to do with the shape that this door was in. Blue light was leaking out all around the edges of the door.

It was dangerous to not have the font contained fully. It was no wonder that the dead were walking in this graveyard. The mere amount of light that seeped out from behind this door would have released enough manna into the ground that could easily have wakened the dead.

Fitting his fingers into one of the cracks around the doorway, he grasped tightly and pulled hard. With less effort than he had imagined, the door came away in his hands, letting the blue energy of the manna within wash over him.

A normal person would have begun screaming immediately from the pain of the horrific mutations that would have started taking over his flesh. Pure manna energy was dangerous, deadly in fact, to naked flesh and those who were not properly attuned.

D'Arden simply felt warm.

Stepping past the ruined threshold, he gazed at the crystalline formation that jutted up sharply from the broken ground. Clear and glowing with blue light, the crystal's energy fountained forth from the center, falling down like mist and light and rolling across the ground. Most would be blinded by now, unable to truly see and appreciate the patterns. He turned to watch the flow as it went across the ground slowly, leisurely, and disappeared into the crypt.

Something was actively funneling the manna. This was more dangerous than he'd realized.

He knelt down near the bubbling energy and thrust his hands into the glow so that they disappeared. He stiffened, never quite used to the feeling of being flooded with the land's life force. Thoughts, feelings, words flowed through his mind in a muddled mess, faster than he could think, faster than he could process. He felt himself being pulled into an infinite blue sea, and he resisted that call, resisted the urge to let himself be swallowed completely by the world.

He clamped his jaw down to keep from screaming as his consciousness touched the corruption. This was small, nothing in comparison to what he knew he would feel when searching the manna in the city, but still it was pure, unbridled agony. It was everything he could do to keep from being absorbed into the stream as the pain weakened his resolve.

The corruption was centered in the crypt. There were

no walking dead in the graveyard because there was a catacomb beneath the mausoleum that housed all of them during the day, so that they would not be dissolved by the light of the rising sun.

There was some kind of malevolent intelligence at work here, but it was not the demon from the city, not the prey he'd been sent after.

With a cry, he pulled his hands from the font. Gasping for air, he slowly rose to his feet. The corruption was not strong here, but he could understand why the captain was concerned. Gazing out over the rows of graves, he noticed that there was no recently disturbed earth, no fresh burial mounds anywhere in sight. He wondered for a moment just what the city had been doing with their dead.

Perhaps it was best that he'd been sent here first. An intelligent guiding of the manna meant one of two things: either the corruption had grown so strong that it had embodied a corpse with a mockery of intelligence, or there was a lesser demon here, orchestrating its own tiny kingdom beneath the soil of sanctified ground.

Which it was, he would have to find out.

He stepped out of the tiny stone chapel and turned to face the doorway once more. With this amount of manna leaking out it could wreak havoc as far away as the city proper. He would have to do something to seal the chapel until he could have it fixed properly.

D'Arden took a few steps backward and closed his eyes. Holding up his arms, he summoned the manna to his fists. The energy diverted from its slow path to the crypt to gather around him, to focus on the two points to which he directed his mind. He felt it building, and he made a few slow movements of his arms, gathering in more of the manna and building it in his center, enhancing his own power in a way that normal men could only dream of doing.

As he felt the energy reach a peak, he thrust his arms forward, propelling the energy away from his body and towards the open doorway of the chapel. With his mind, he constructed a solid wall of energy where the door had stood, shaping it and hewing it from the rawness of the manna.

When once more he opened his eyes, there was a wall of solid blackness between him and the energy of the font that allowed no ray of light, no drop of energy to escape. The manna still flowed across the ground towards the crypt – there was no way that he could cut off a directed flow – but at least no more of the unsuspecting dead would be rousted from their eternal sleep.

That would do for now.

He drew the crystalline blade from his back, and it came free from its specially-designed scabbard with a low rasp. He turned towards the crypt and began a slow stride across the dead, packed earth.

The door of the mausoleum was tightly sealed. No wonder, he thought, with so many creatures which would be instantly returned to their state of death if they were caught in the sunlight.

He could only hope that some would be so destroyed when he forced the door open.

Tactics similar to those that had removed the obstacles at the blocked entrance to the font chapel proved useless. He was unable to pry the door open by physical means, no matter how much strength he put behind it. He simply could not get enough leverage on the door in order to wrench it free from its holdings.

D'Arden sighed.

A few moments later, the door to the mausoleum exploded inward, followed by licks of the azure force that had driven it forward.

Nothing stood directly in the doorway. It was a pity.

He stepped over shards of shattered stone as he crossed the threshold. He could feel the corruption here, now – it washed over him as it was freed from the confines of the crypt, red and cold and dangerous and twisted, causing his spirit to recoil in horror. Something was very wrong here.

Cautiously he moved into the darkness, the soft blue light that dripped from his sword illuminating the path before him. There was no movement in the narrow stone passageway before him.

He took another step forward.

Something lurched at him out of the darkness, releasing a dried, decaying moan. A corpse stumbled towards him as he stepped backward, its arms outstretched. He could see it in the cobalt light of the manna blade, its skin parchment-dry and cracking, barely covering the bone in some places, no eyes left in the sockets, staring at him with a long-empty gaze. Red points of light glowed angrily within those deep empty holes, the life gone forever from this empty shell which was animated only by the twisted, perverted manna that dwelled within.

He swung his blade in a perfect arc at the walking corpse, severing it in two at the waist. The blue fire licked forth from the blade as it cut through dried flesh and shattered decaying bone, engulfing the rotted flesh as it consumed and purified the manna within.

The abomination collapsed into dust and bones, and

then those too were quickly returned to the land as the manna consumed it all.

Corrupted manna took many forms; there were natural snarls in it that would cause beasts and men to change their form and become hideous monsters, like the fel dogs in the forest. Demons could manipulate the manna to create whatever horrific images they could imagine. D'Arden had battled against many different foes, even through one demon's image of inferno itself, but still he could not stop himself from being unsettled by the sight of walking corpses.

It was not going to get any better in the foreseeable future.

He suppressed a shudder.

The small corridor that made up the entry gave way into a large inner chamber, with several stones reading different names upon each one. This was obviously not the mausoleum for just one family, but perhaps for all of the gentry of Calessa, marking the burial places of the rich and the decadent, who now likely once again walked the catacombs beneath him as a shadow of their lives, a mockery of life and everything precious and dear within it.

He held up his crystalline sword like a torch, using it to read the names of those etched forever in stone. Some were so faded that he could not read them at all, others seemed fairly fresh, bodies of the dead inhumed so recently as the past year or two. The names were long, flowing, and reminiscent of poetry, a reflection of the upper class that the bodies had once belonged to.

In the dim azure light, he spotted the stairwell that descended to the catacombs, where would be resting the bodies of the richest of the rich, the patrons and matrons of great familial dynasties, each likely entombed in their own gold-plated sarcophagus, with scripted lines of expensive writing etched on plaques attached to each. Rest in peace indeed... rest forever in the same decadence that they lived their entire lives.

Cautiously, he approached the staircase. If the manna could be sensed by smell, this place would be stinking of corruption. Instead, there was only the sickly sweet scent of death permeating the air.

A soft light came up the stairs from below. It was almost undetectable from the top of the steps, but he could see it if he focused his eyes clearly. There was someone – or something – down there.

Slowly, carefully, he began to descend the steps. He knew not what might await him at the bottom; he could be mobbed with the reanimated flesh of the long-dead and wasted away... or perhaps something even worse.

His foot touched down on what his mind told him was the final step. He stooped slightly and held his sword at the ground, letting the soft blue light confirm his suspicions – he had reached the bottom.

D'Arden looked around sharply. Nothing came flying at him from the darkness, nor any unexpected attacks from the rotting flesh of the undead.

This, of course, only served to make him more suspicious.

He stood in what seemed to be a great hall of some kind. The stairs had descended further than he had realized. The ceiling was high, raised up so far that the light from the manna blade could not illuminate the stone that lay above him. To the left of him and to the right there were no walls to be found within easy reach. He wondered just how large this catacomb might be, just how far in each direction that it might stretch. There was no telling from his limited sight.

It seemed to him that the dim glow he'd seen from the top of the stairs must have been an illusion of some kind, a trick to lure him down into the depths of danger. In fact, though, when he placed the sword behind his back to dim the light that shone in front of him, he could almost make it out – a soft, warm light somewhere ahead of him, in what appeared to be the distance.

He took a cautious step forward, and then another. There was no sound, no inkling that anything living had set foot down here in many years. Not even a rat scurried, so silent was the tomb that he found himself in.

At that thought, he couldn't help but swallow hard. He'd not intended for this mausoleum to become his tomb.

The only sounds that he could hear were the pounding of his heartbeat in his ears and his shallow, rapid breathing. He took another step forward, and another, feeling as though he were following a path into oblivion with only the dim light of the manna in his blade to guide him. The light shone no truth, no revelations on this darkness that enveloped him and seemed to consume the very light from his soul.

He dared not speak aloud, lest it give those who dwelt this far beneath the soil some advantage over him. If they were not already aware of his presence from the disturbance he'd wreaked on the manna above him, then they were preoccupied at least. He'd have hoped for a more stealthy approach to entering the crypt, but he knew that anything which would purposely manipulate the manna in this way would have sensed him coming when he'd first set foot on the graveyard.

He reached a point in the darkness where he could no longer tell whether he was still standing in the same chamber. The wall behind him had vanished into the black, and on all sides of him there was nothing. He felt as though he were an island of existence, as if all of creation had simply been washed away around him, leaving him standing perfectly alone in the remaining oblivion.

Something brushed his right shoulder.

He spun around sharply, bringing the crystalline blade around in a flashing downward arc. He felt the blade meet flesh, then bone, and something moaned and stumbled away from him. In the flash of azure light as the manna fire caught the corrupted and dusty flesh aflame, he saw them.

They seemed to be almost innumerable, the number of animated dead that surrounded him. He only caught glimpses of their horrid faces in the light of the fire – they'd been quiet, oh, so quiet – the empty eyes, the desiccated faces, the yawning gulfs where once had been facial features. His breath came in a short gasp.

Then they came.

They came at him in a wave, a gasping, breathless wave of angry dead, roused from their eternal sleep in the most horrific way possible. He lay about him with his blade, hacking through the ranks of the corpses that came at him from all sides, lighting them afire as the pure manna that flowed within him and his sword sought desperately to purify the incredible corruption around them. They clawed at his eyes with shrunken fingers, pawed at his cloak and sought to drag him down beneath a sea of rotted flesh.

His breathing heightened even more as he ducked,

weaved and tore himself from the grasp of the horrid things. In their grasping claws they took bits of cloth, leather and flesh as he cut them down, one by one. In some cases the manna fire leapt from one standing corpse to another, or a group of several would be devoured by the purifying cobalt flames.

Then, they were gone.

He stood alone once more, his only fleeting companions the wisps of manna fire that quickly vanished once more into the darkness as the dust and bones clattered to the ground and disappeared forever, returned to the flow of life from the earth. There was a swelling of manna here now – when a man died and the flesh slowly rotted, the life force would be returned to the earth slowly, in time, so as not to cause a buildup of manna too great which could cause a new font to spring up spontaneously... or worse, create a snarl that would create some sort of hideous new creature.

Panting, he fell to one knee. He could feel blood trickling from several minor wounds, but he could not identify a mortal wound anywhere on his body, or even a dangerous one. The swarm of corpses had nearly driven him to the ground, and he would have had no recourse left in the dark... if they'd gotten his sword away from him too, all could have been lost.

The sound of slow applause drew his attention. It was a dry sound, with none of the moisture of the applause of men. He shuddered at the sound, a twisted mockery of the appreciative sound made by the living.

"I am truly humbled by that display," said a thin, rough voice from the darkness.

A figure stepped forward, ringed in a dull red light

that illuminated a visage not unlike the other corpses which he had just fought. In the pinpoints of light within the empty skull though, D'Arden could see not only the angry red light of corruption, but a firey light that told a story all too clear.

The corrupted manna had created life – life out of death.

"Your existence is a lie," D'Arden snarled, regaining his feet. "You are nothing but a construct of evil, of darkness."

"The manna is both good and evil, light and dark, Arbiter," the corpse rasped. "It created you, and it created me. Even that which you worship as pure will cause men to scream and die unless properly treated." A horrific image stretched across its face that might have once been a grin. "Unless they are created… like you."

"I will return you to oblivion," D'Arden said calmly, leveling his blade at the creature. "You have no right to walk this land."

"Admittedly, you have verily decimated my army of the undead, Arbiter," it said, with what might have been a hint of humor in its centuries-old voice. "But no matter. There are still corpses here that remain yet cold, bodies of those which might still be put to good use, once you are destroyed. Perhaps… even yours."

With a snarl of rage, D'Arden leapt forward, swinging his blade out in a deadly arc. The corpse jerked like a puppet whose master had pulled too hard on its strings and moved aside too quickly for his strike to make a connection.

It laughed, a sound that resembled tearing parchment. "Strike a nerve, did I, Arbiter? You do not wish to join my army of the everlasting?"

Without answering, he brought the blade around in an upward arc, slashing viciously. As he did, he released one hand off of the hilt of the crystal blade and thrust it outward sharply, delivering a blast of azure force that very nearly connected with the corpse and would have consumed it there and then, but missed narrowly and splashed harmlessly against the stone floor a few feet away, instantly vanishing.

"Your skills are lacking," the corpse taunted. "How many beasts have you slain, Arbiter, and yet you cannot defeat me?"

"I shall defeat you!" D'Arden said, driving his crystal blade forward in a powerful thrust.

The creature almost seemed to vanish before his very eyes before reappearing a few arm's lengths away. "Too slow, Arbiter. Come, destroy me! Send my corruption back to the earth! Purify this place, if you can!"

D'Arden made another cutting attack, but once again, his strike fell short. The creature shook its head – a motion that threatened to dislodge the skull from its perilous perch atop the decayed shoulders – and sighed heavily.

"Very well," it gasped. "If you cannot defeat me, then I will defeat you!"

Red light began to build up around the corpse as it drew the corrupted manna inward. D'Arden fell a step backward – it had been many months since he'd faced down a construct so powerful, and he found himself almost in awe of the horrible sight before his eyes.

"Now die!" the corpse breathed.

The corrupted manna shot forth from the skeletal fingers in long, sinewy ropes. One looped itself around his sword arm, the other attaching itself to his left ankle. Immediately he pulled taut against them, trying to pull the corpse off balance and within reach of a fatal strike, but his efforts proved in vain.

"Do not take me for such a weakling," the beast said, sending out two more tendrils that wrapped around his other arm and neck. They tightened, and suddenly D'Arden found it difficult to breathe. "You've lost, Arbiter. I'm going to snap your puny, fragile neck and use your corpse to eat the citizens of that city alive!"

D'Arden pulled hard against the magical bonds, and then rolled himself over his shoulder directly at the corpse, bringing up his sword in a sharp arc as there was suddenly slack available. The thing shrieked and pulled backwards, cackling dryly as it pulled the bonds tightly around him once again.

"Good try, but not enough!" it laughed.

He closed his eyes as the bonds tightened around them. He was beginning to feel dizzy from lack of air, and the agony of the pressure on his windpipe was making him desperately want to cough. He could feel the strength being sapped out of him as he struggled in vain against them.

There was no way to breathe and draw the manna inward. His sword hand was immobilized.

Expelling what little remained of his breath, he focused all of the manna remaining within him on his right hand – his all-important sword hand. If only he could get that free, he might escape this grisly demise. Power collected around his wrist, and he focused the entirety of his will on that single spot.

For an instant, the bonds loosened.

An instant was all he needed.

Immediately he yanked his hand free and cut through the glowing rope holding his neck in a single stroke. It separated at the point of contact and the blue flames leapt forth from the sword, traveling quickly down the severed connection towards the living corpse. It shrieked and dropped the connection immediately, loosening the rest of the bonds attached to him.

He drew in a breath, the death-scented air tasting sweeter than any other.

"It's time for this to end," D'Arden gasped, charging forward.

The corpse seemed stunned by the fact that he'd escaped the deathtrap that he'd fallen into, and barely moved as he brought the sword up, separating the desiccated skull from the shoulders. The skull flew through the air and hit the ground some feet away – D'Arden could hear the powdery crack as it struck the stone floor with enough force to shatter it.

The manna fire leapt from the point of contact and began devouring the dry and dusty corpse. There was no shriek, no sound of protest as the blue fire burned almost brightly enough to illuminate what appeared to be a truly massive chamber.

When the corpse was gone, the fire leapt outward still, through the air with nothing to keep it afloat, purifying the corrupted lines of manna that flowed through here and were caught in the corpse's web. D'Arden breathed slowly and smoothly as much of it flowed through him as a vessel for purification, passing through his spirit and his body in its search for purity. It was a blissful agony, one he always endured.

The fire popped and crackled in the air around him just as it burned in his veins. His muscles strained against the misery inflicted by the massive amount of corruption that needed purifying, and worse, the knowledge that it would only remain pure for so long, unless he was able to find the demon in the city and destroy it once and for all.

He let out a long, low cry of pain.

When finally the pain subsided, he fell to his knees. The crystal sword dropped from his hand, and immediately its light was extinguished as the contact from his flesh was broken. It clattered to the floor, forgotten as he struggled to draw breath through his damaged throat.

All was dark.

His mind slowly returned to normal as he felt the collection of manna begin ebbing into the earth. The twist that had caused the corruption had been unraveled, and now the manna would begin flowing back in its usual patterns. The lasting effect still might drive up a font here, but if that were the case he'd simply have the citizens of Calessa board up the mausoleum and build a new one so that there would be no chance of anyone being harmed by accidentally venturing down here.

He picked up the manna blade, and it immediately lit up once more, buoyed again by the life force flowing through his veins. It was his torch as he made his way back across the stone floor and up the steep stairway, back towards the light of outside and the haven of civilization.

It was time the guard captain gave him what he wanted.

II
CALESSA HEIGHTS

"You look like hell," Captain Mor observed.

D'Arden had returned from the graveyard looking somewhat the worse for wear. Angry red burns festered on his wrists and his neck and, he supposed, his ankles, where the beast's corrupted manna had held him fast. He bore them proudly, though not without pain. He suspected the one around his neck might leave a ringed scar that could stay, possibly forever.

"A most astute observation, Captain," D'Arden said dryly. "Now, about our arrangement? Your cemetery has been cleansed... the beast that dwelt within the depths of the crypt no longer walks."

"Of course, of course," the Captain said. "I'd take you there myself, but I've got a watch to attend to. I'll summon one of the soldiers on duty now in the area to take you to the chapel. Just make sure that he doesn't get any of that stuff on him... I can't have my men turning into fel beasts."

"I believe we can manage that," the Arbiter said.

"Mikel!" the Captain thundered. Another soldier, one D'Arden did not recognize, quickly entered the room. He was young, fresh-faced, barely into his facial hair – D'Arden guessed he was no more than sixteen winters old. "Take the Arbiter to the font chapel nearby. Make sure you're standing clear out of the way, boy... I don't want to be the one to put you down if you turn into some ravening, flesh-eating lunatic."

The boy swallowed visibly. "Y...yes, sir."

D'Arden exchanged an amused look with the captain. He found himself liking the man, despite his initial impressions. Mor seemed to have a good head on his shoulders, and a sense of humor to boot.

"F...follow me, if you will, master Arbiter," Mikel said.

D'Arden suppressed a chuckle as he followed the lad out of the barracks and onto the street. It was light out, now, and the merchants were on the streets in force. The sun was casting everything in a warm light, but there was nothing warm about the day. A bitter chill ran through the air and he guessed that the temperatures would have frozen standing water inside of a few moments. Still, there was little water to be seen – there were no clouds in the sky and no chance of rain or snow. He wondered how these people had survived for so long with no falling water.

"The font chapel is this way," the lad said, pointing down one of the streets.

D'Arden could see the front of it now, nestled amongst the other buildings. Font chapels had to be built wherever the font sprang up – they had to be contained immediately, lest they begin wreaking havoc amongst the populace. If that meant destroying wings of ancient buildings and relocating housing and storefronts, then that's what was done. There was never any question or protests when a manna font sprung up – it was just the way of life.

The streets were empty here, and the buildings all deserted for a block around the chapel. No one wanted to be near the thing.

Mikel stopped several yards from the front door of the chapel and held out the small silver key that would unlock the door. "Here you are, master Arbiter. I've been instructed to wait for you out here, but I won't get any closer than this if you're going to be opening that door."

D'Arden grimaced. "I've no choice, lad."

"I know," the boy said simply.

With a small sigh, D'Arden approached the wooden door that was barred and locked from the outside. No one would ever dare lock a manna font chapel from the inside – it would be the last thing they ever did before they were swallowed by the earth.

Checking over both shoulders, D'Arden unlocked the door and swung out the hinged metal bar that provided the primary method of holding it shut. The thing was so heavily fortified that it seemed as though it would take an army to break in without the blessing of the city's guard captain.

Opening the door no more than a crack, he slipped inside and closed it shut behind him.

The manna within blinded him. It was so twisted, so foul that he could almost smell it, taste it, hear the screaming of the tortured earth. It filled all of his senses with hatred and rage and pain and enduring torment that he nearly let out a cry of his own to match. There was no calming blue light of purity here, only the crimson of corruption and anger and evil.

Barely able to bite back the pain he suddenly found himself in, he took the three short steps to the center of the chapel and thrust his hands into the crystalline font. If what had been before was unbearable, this was simply impossible. He was almost shredded alive by that which lay within.

There was corruption everywhere here. There was

perhaps not a square inch of the city which was not completely confounded by evil. He was awestruck for a moment that there were not manna fonts littering every street corner of this god-forsaken place with the amount of twisted life-force that was buried beneath the frozen soil. It was immediately apparent to him why there was no life here – no plants, no living trees, and no snow on the ground or clouds in the sky. It was all being absorbed into the earth and twisted by something that was far more powerful than anything he had ever encountered in his twenty-seven winters as a living being, and far more dangerous than anything he'd ever imagined in his worst nightmares.

With a soft cry, he pulled his hands free of the pool. He staggered backwards and sagged heavily against the inside of the door, but only for a moment. As quickly as he could find the strength, he pushed the door open and stumbled out, slamming it behind him and hauling the metal bars back across it, thrusting the key back into the lock and twisting it closed. He sagged against the wooden door, sliding downward until he was sitting upon the ground, exhausted.

"Master Arbiter!" the boy called, clearly unsure whether it was safe to approach.

"Not yet!" he gasped. "Not yet! The manna has not yet faded! Do not come near me until I say otherwise!"

Although pure manna was dangerous to men, corrupted manna was worse. It could immediately enslave a normal man to the will of whatever was controlling it – it could transform a man into something beyond fathoming, or it could simply annihilate his soul and leave him an empty vessel for something much worse to come along and inhabit the empty shell the soul left behind. He would not allow any such thing to happen to anyone here.

Of course, it was likely that there were already some to which it had happened.

He sighed heavily as he felt the last of the energy fade away. There was no way that he could read the manna in order to determine the location of the demon. The land was already too far gone here, and it could be of little help to him now. He would have to rely on his own intuition and investigating skills to determine where it could be hiding.

The difficult thing with demons was that they were extremely intelligent, cunning and often had powers of illusion.

Exhausted, he waved over the young soldier who had escorted him here. "It's all right, lad. It's fine now."

The boy took a few hesitant steps, and then his strides became more purposeful as he closed the gap between them. The lad knelt down beside him. "Are you all right, master Arbiter?"

"I'll be fine," D'Arden said, the last word turning into a choking cough.

After he had recovered, D'Arden looked the boy in the eye. "I may need your help, lad. There's a lot going on in this city, and I'm sure it's more than you'd ever care to know. Let me tell you what I know right now; the corruption in this place is simply beyond fathoming. The demon that's caused this has been here for months, or perhaps even years, living somewhere in the city and causing all of the manna to twist and become unbearable complicated. I could have an army of Arbiters and we might not be able to purify this place on our own without finding and destroying the demon.

"Tell me, boy… from where have the worst reports of those affected come?"

The soldier named Mikel hesitated for a moment, clearly unsure whether he should be sharing that information with a total stranger without the captain's prior approval. After a moment, though, he brightened and said, "From the high quarter, m'lord. That's where the worst of it's been, though the folk up there don't like to talk about it."

D'Arden nodded. The young soldier could certainly prove to be useful in his investigation. Bright, obviously brave, and willing to give him information that the captain might not be so forthcoming with. "Thank you, lad."

"Please, m'lord… call me Mikel."

"Of course, Mikel. Will you escort me to the high quarter? I will need to have a look around if we're to have any hope of finding this beast and bringing life back to Calessa." D'Arden gestured around at the city.

"It's been this way for years, m'lord," Mikel said. "To be honest, hardly any of us are ever expecting it to go back to the way it used to be. We're used to it now."

"Much longer and there won't be anyone left to be used to anything," D'Arden muttered. "Where does your family live, Mikel?"

"They all live down in the low quarter, master Arbiter," he replied. "I became a soldier, joined in with the captain to give them all a better life. Not much of a life we have here anyways, but at least we can afford to buy food."

"You're doing right by them, lad," D'Arden said, his words carefully calculated to endear himself to the boy. "I'm always glad to see a boy become a soldier and protect his family. It's a hard choice to make, but it's the right one if you have it."

Mikel nodded. "It's hard being a soldier, but it's good for them, and it makes my father happy."

"Have there been many problems with the corruption in the low quarter, where your family lives?" D'Arden asked.

The boy shook his head. "Not many. There's a few that we've had to…" the boy swallowed hard, "…put down, but not too many. One was a neighbor of my family… he just turned one day, started howling about how he was going to eat their flesh off their bones." He shuddered. "It was horrible, but the captain, he sent some soldiers down and they took care of things."

"They didn't hurt your family?"

"No."

D'Arden nodded. "That's good."

"Up in the high quarter, though, they all got their windows and doors boarded up. They hardly ever come out anymore. They got animals up there gone feral, and men and women locked up in their houses, scrabbling at the insides, trying to get out so they can go out and start killing. It's a madhouse up there – the captain keeps saying we should just board up and quarantine the whole quarter, but there's still men alive up there who won't leave. We can't just leave them up there."

It would probably be better for everyone if you did, D'Arden thought, but did not say it aloud. Instead, he said, "It could be dangerous. Are you sure you want to come along with me?"

Steadfastly, the boy nodded.

Good then. Perhaps he could earn the boy's loyalty

yet.

"Come then, Mikel. Lead the way to the high quarter. We'll go see what we can do. Perhaps we'll find the demon this morning."

Somehow, that didn't appear to reassure the boy.

They ventured through the city streets. D'Arden had expected throngs of people to fill them, but instead he found them mostly desolate and empty. There was some noise coming from the trade quarter, the section of the city they'd left behind, but there was little noise as they passed by street after street in the central city. Storefronts lay abandoned, homes were despondent-looking and empty, and there was a pervasive feeling of fear and anxiety looming in the air. Even in the warm light of the sun everything seemed cold, lonely and lifeless. A few faces peered out at them from windows, and though while they did not seem to be the ravening beasts that might have been created from the corruption, they were clearly afraid of both what was happening to their home, and of him.

"How can you touch the manna?" the boy asked idly as they walked along the deserted streets. "If it kills everyone else it touches, how is it that it doesn't kill you?"

D'Arden sighed, trying to determine the best way to answer that deceptively complex question. "Do you know much about the Arbiters?"

"Not much," the boy said. "Only a little, that there used to be a lot more of them, and they were the enforcers of the law back in the old days."

"That's almost right," D'Arden said. "The Arbiters were created by the Last King in the days of the empire to serve his will. They were an organization then, a group of those dedicated to protect the manna from turning evil. There are so many ways that it can happen. So, the best and the brightest sorcerers were given the chance to become Arbiters, to protect the world against the corruption.

"When they realized that even though they were great sorcerers, they were still just men and subject to the power of the manna just like everyone else, they knew that something would have to be done. There would have to be someone who could touch the manna, not just see it.

"So, in order to do that, there were great experiments done to determine how men could be immunized against the power of the manna. A great many men, women and children died in the search of that end, until they discovered the way."

He recited the formula from memory, the same words that had been told to him all those years ago. When he had heard them the first time, they had affixed themselves to his memory in a way that he knew would never fade, not even if he were to live one hundred winters. "To create an Arbiter, a person must be exposed to the manna over a period of several years, in extremely small doses. These must be administered directly to the heart of the person who is being ordained, via a small, rounded blade – known as the heartblade – that is slipped between the ribs and used to touch the heart. Over time, the dosage grows, and eventually a resistance is attained." They sounded as cold, as clinical to him now as they had the first time he'd heard them. "This process never ends; we must be regularly exposed directly to the manna via the heartblade." The ritual, though at first painful and terrifying, was now little more than drinking a glass of water to him, although slightly more painful.

Mikel' eyes were wide as he listened to the story. "So… you have to stab yourself in the heart over and over again?"

"That's exactly right," D'Arden said.

"Why would you do something like that?"

"There are many reasons, lad. One is because the world is a dangerous place, and it needs people who are willing to sacrifice themselves to protect it. Another is because my life would be meaningless without this purpose to drive it forward. Mostly, it is because there are those out there who would seek to corrupt the world, and I do not intend to let something like that happen. My pain and my strength are my sacrifice to help keep the land a little safer from those who would seek to do it harm."

"That's awful," Mikel said.

"Perhaps, but it is the truth," D'Arden said. "Sometimes the truth is horrifying."

"I don't think I could ever do something like that," Mikel said.

"You likely could not," D'Arden replied. "The reason that most Arbiters are started at a very young age is because it is so that the manna begins its effects on them while they are still malleable, while their souls are still able to be touched by the power without it destroying them. Starting when one is older is far more difficult, and not in the least because the heartblade is excruciatingly painful at first. Some Arbiters, when they go too long without being exposed to the heartblade as they are supposed to, go quite mad."

"Do you think that's what happened to the one that came here a few years ago?" the boy asked.

D'Arden frowned. He didn't know how to answer that

question. He wasn't certain how he could tell the boy that no matter what he'd told the captain, there was a chance that it was that very Arbiter that was either the force responsible for this entire miserable catastrophe here in the city, or that he could be very well working with the demon. There were too many unknowns here, some of which he hoped to resolve with this trip to the most dangerous part of the city.

It wasn't long before D'Arden and the boy stood before the gate. The boy stopped a few steps before they passed under the arch, clearly hesitant to proceed any further. D'Arden slowed to a halt only a few steps ahead of Mikel and stared up at the great stone structure.

CALESSA HEIGHTS, read the spindly, gothic lettering that adorned the front of the city gate. It was similar the one he'd passed through upon entering the city, but for the lack of the heavy wooden doors that kept out intruders from the outside. The gate itself appeared normal enough, but it was when his eyes ventured out into the city beyond the portal that he felt a chill run down his spine.

Clearly it was not long ago that this area was the richest part of the city. There was still a feeling of wealth that pervaded the design and decorations on the buildings, and yet everything had fallen into ruin. Despite the cheerful and bright adornments around windows and doorways, all of them were faded and tattered. The place looked little better than a slum. D'Arden guessed that the slums might, in fact, look nicer than this place.

"It's a horrid place," Mikel said with a shudder. "Not many go in and out of here anymore. Even the soldiers avoid it. For some reason, most of the beasts stay inside… none of us are quite sure why. When one does get out, it's always at night – and we always have guards posted outside at night to keep them in."

D'Arden knew exactly why the fel beasts stayed inside the gate.

There was already plenty to feed on.

"They won't stay in there forever," D'Arden said solemnly. "Once the food supply runs out in there, they'll be coming out, searching for sustenance."

"The food supply?" Mikel said. "There hasn't been any supplies going into there in months."

D'Arden simply looked at the boy, his manna-blue eyes searching for the light of understanding. After a moment, it seemed to dawn on Mikel, and he looked horrified. "You... you can't mean..."

"I'm afraid I do," the Arbiter said.

"We have to do something! You mean there are still people in there?"

"Most likely," D'Arden said grimly. "Although I would imagine that not many are left, if this has been going on for months. It's likely that any we were to rescue now would be long lost from the reaches of sanity."

Mikel's complexion had taken on a bit of a green tint, but D'Arden found that he had little sympathy for the boy. They lived in a horrid place, in terrible times, and it confounded him how this young soldier could have clung to his innocence for so long. D'Arden had no choice but to give the parents some credit... to raise a child so naïve in a place like this would have taken devoted parenting.

"What did you expect, boy?" D'Arden asked, finding his voice harsher than he'd intended. "That we would simply ride in there and save the day? That it would be simple, straightforward, that we could enter this living hell

50

and rescue those who might be left alive, and they would be perfectly fine and grateful for our help?" He shook his head. "Those are tales for children. Things don't happen like that in this world. We'll be lucky if we find anyone beyond this gate who isn't dead or already turned into one of those horrid beasts, but if we do, it's a near certainty that they'll be stark raving mad at best."

"Then… why do we want to go in there at all?" Mikel said. "If there's no one left to rescue…"

"We go in there not to rescue, not to save the lives that are already lost," D'Arden said. "We proceed beyond this gate only because a concentration of fel beasts so high likely means that this will be either the demon's hiding place, or his source of energy. Either way, we stand to discover valuable clues regarding its whereabouts, and that is the most important task right now."

Mikel swallowed hard and drew his sword. The steel rung loudly in the still air as the shining blade came forth from its resting place. He held it a bit unsteadily, as though he were well trained but only in drills. D'Arden doubted if he'd even taken a life before in his short time.

"Have you ever used that blade?" the Arbiter asked.

"Only in drills," the boy answered, confirming his suspicions.

"Are you ready to use it today?"

Only for a moment did Mikel hesitate. "I am."

"Good," D'Arden said. "Because you're going to need it."

Together, they took the first step across the threshold into Calessa Heights.

**

51

The streets were desolate and lonely in the high quarter of the city. Dust blew in the wind, stirring up into small devils and then quickly settling again before picking up once more a few feet away. There were no sounds except for the rustling of their cloth and the sounds of their feet against the cobblestones. The ornately designed buildings were dusty and bedraggled, seeming almost to be relics of a lost age. In a way, D'Arden thought, perhaps they were.

Here and there could be seen a bloodstain – on the ground, perhaps across a doorway, or smeared on the side of a building. They were always long dried, and never fresh. He wondered how it was that there seemed to be no life here at all, and yet there clearly had been only a few months previous. He could almost imagine the children playing in the streets, mothers calling out from the houses for their precious babes and they would come running home just in time for dinner. Instead, the only sounds that seemed to echo in these streets were the cries and screams of the damned, and though he heard nothing, he could swear that the agony of death was palpable everywhere he looked.

"It's so quiet," Mikel whispered. "Where is everyone?"

"Either dead," D'Arden said in a low tone, "Or perhaps contributing to the body count. We must find where the fel beasts are hiding. This may be difficult for you, boy – I know none of the folk here, but you do. There may be faces that you recognize. Know that they are no longer the people you knew, but simply monsters wearing their image. You must cut them down quickly and decisively, because if you do not, they will feast on your flesh and dig out your eyes with their bare hands."

"How will I know who is dangerous and who is not?" Mikel said.

"Demons are clever and cunning, but fel beasts are not. They know nothing except the hunger to kill and destroy. If any one of them speaks so much as a word to you that is not a black curse or a cry of hunger, then stay your hand. Otherwise, be sure that you strike first." D'Arden kept his voice level. He could feel that the strain on the young man was beginning to take its toll on his mind.

"Can't the manna tell you where they're hiding?" Mikel asked.

D'Arden shook his head. "It's too far gone. The corruption is too great here. I cannot read the manna right now, no more than you could read information by staring directly into the sun. All it would do is cause you agony and burn your eyes so they could no longer see."

Across the street, D'Arden spotted what looked like a corpse. "Stay close, boy. Follow me and keep an eye out for anything that might be on the prowl."

Mikel nodded grimly, and they crossed together. D'Arden was right – it was the corpse of a small girl child, no more than seven winters old when she'd died. The kill was not fresh, but it was recent. No smell of decay marked the flesh, nor had it begun to swell in the light of the sun. The flesh was cold and hard, and the eyes stared sightlessly upward, as though they were unwilling to gaze upon the horrific gash that had torn open her throat and stained the pretty green dress she wore dark with her own blood. It was almost as though someone with a particularly dark sense of humor had sculpted a porcelain doll and left it lying thoughtlessly in the street, so pale was the child's graying flesh.

D'Arden stole a glance at the boy, who was staring studiously away from the body. The Arbiter guessed that Mikel had seen his fair share of death, but he understood how difficult it could be to see such a horrific fate come to a child. He reached out one hand to close the girl's eyes.

The dead girl seemed to come suddenly to life as her teeth closed on his wrist. He gave a sharp cry as the child's sharp incisors drew blood, and as he yanked his hand away, his flesh tore apart, dripping scarlet across the road and adding to the darkness on the child's dress.

"Mikel!" D'Arden shouted.

The steel blade flashed in the sunlight and connected with the child's corpse as it leapt into the air toward the Arbiter's throat. There was no spray of blood as there might have been if the blade had cut living flesh, but instead it simply cut a heavy gash at the corpse's midsection. The body no longer had the support to keep itself upright and collapsed onto the cobblestones, but still it clawed towards them even as they took a large step backwards.

"Stand back, boy," D'Arden said, holding his injured wrist close to his body. With his other hand, he collected the manna around it – dangerous, with so much corruption around – drawing the power from within him rather than from without to avoid feeding the creature further with corrupted power, and shot a bolt of azure light at the animated corpse. It let out a terrible, rasping shriek as the manna fire engulfed the body and consumed it to nothing within the space of a few seconds.

"What… what was that?" the boy gasped, staggering backwards.

"Exactly what it looked like," D'Arden said with a

grimace. The pain in his wrist lanced through his body as the manna purified the corruption that remained behind from the child's teeth. "You came through with that sword, boy. I'm impressed with that swing. If you hadn't, I'm not sure I could have gotten my blade up in time, and then the beast would have been at my throat."

"But... that child..." Mikel stuttered.

"Yes, the child. The child that hasn't been a child for quite some time. Who knows how long she may have been lying there, just waiting for you or one of your companions to cross the gate and attempt to come to her aid. It's the corruption, boy. It's all around you, it's everywhere... and it spares no one from its horror."

D'Arden checked his wrist. The wound had already begun to knit itself back together, and blood no longer seeped forth from the torn flesh. The manna was in his veins, in his blood, and he could already see the little wisps of blue fire that crept along the ground from the scarlet drops that had fallen, seeking out the corrupted manna and purifying what little of it was present. He flexed the healing joint once, twice and then nodded sharply.

"It appears it may be more dangerous here than I thought," D'Arden said, reaching his hand back behind his shoulder and grasping the handle of his crystalline blade. With its characteristic rasp, it came free from its holding, the blue glow pulsing slightly as it immediately sprang to life.

Mikel stared at the crystal sword with wide eyes. "That's a manna blade. Is it dangerous?"

"Not to any but those who are cut by its edge," D'Arden answered. "It does not radiate uncontrolled power like the fonts do. Every drop of power within this blade is controlled carefully by me, and none escapes without my explicit direction."

The boy let out the breath he had been holding. "That's good."

D'Arden glanced around them in both directions. The child had been the only person on the street. Everything else was silent, desolate, lonely. He did see, though, that on the far side of the street there was a door to a richly decorated building that hung slightly ajar, revealing only darkness within.

He raised one hand to sight along it, extending one finger in a gesture of indication. "There. That is where we go next. We must determine where the demon's source of power is, and whether these folk are only his food, or whether he dwells among them, perhaps forcing them to venerate him as some sort of sick, twisted deity."

"Do demons do that often?" the boy asked.

"Perhaps too often," D'Arden said.

They crossed the street and approached the open doorway. D'Arden slowed his pace considerably once they reached within a few steps of the arch, holding out one hand behind him to indicate that his armored companion should slow his gait as well. Carefully, cautiously, he crept closer to the aperture, listening intently for any sounds that might emit from within.

Only silence issued forth.

Holding his hand out behind him once more to indicate that the boy should stay where he was, D'Arden pushed open the thick wooden door. Its hinges let out a creak so loud that it felt for a moment as if the silent world had been torn asunder.

Damn. Now, if there was anything inside, they would

know for certain that he was coming. It seemed to be his luck these days.

Suddenly tiring of stealth, D'Arden shoved open the door, allowing the sapphire light from his blade to illuminate the darkened interior.

He was greeted with only more darkness.

D'Arden stepped carefully across the threshold. Sorcerers could do terrible things with the manna when they tried, and he had come to find himself extremely cautious when crossing a doorway. They could lay traps that would explode violently when triggered, and they would do it with abandon. A man who dared to use the manna, who had a will strong enough to control it without falling immediately before its grace and majesty, was a dangerous animal – and nearly always fell victim to their own corruption. Sorcerers were often in league with demons, for whatever reason. Promises of wealth, power, sometimes even of eternal dominion over the land itself… promises that were always broken, never fulfilled.

In a place this corrupted, there could be a sorcerer hiding around any corner.

What he found within was obviously once a carefully-decorated entryway to a home. Cloaks hung on the wall and there were boots piled along the floor, lying haphazardly, strewn in every direction. A layer of dust had settled upon them; they had not been used, nor even disturbed in some time. The same layer of dust covered the floor, and there were no recent footprints. This place might not have any relevance at all to the demon's whereabouts.

A sound – a low, aching moan – came from within. He immediately stopped moving, unsure if perhaps it had been made by one of the floorboards beneath his feet. When he heard it again, longer this time and slightly louder, he knew that there was someone... or something within.

He moved swiftly and smoothly across the floor, pressing his back against the wall as he reached the next doorway that would take him inside to the house proper. It was dangerous to investigate, he knew, but if the boy outside got wind that there was someone inside and he didn't properly determine whether said person was still human in this awful place or not, he would have a very small, manageable mutiny on his hands, but one that would still be quite unfortunate.

The next door was slightly open also, and D'Arden shone the light from his blade through the small opening. There was rich furniture within, all covered with the same layer of dust. That same sound, the low, sad cry issued once more from beyond the nearly closed portal. It was a sound of pain, a sound of mourning. D'Arden felt his hackles go up. It was not uncommon for a fel beast to feign death or near-death in order to lure its prey close enough so that it could reach out and feed when one approached just one step too far. The child had been one of those, and he'd seen many before. The loved ones of a man would come home to find him crying out in pain and with desperate pleas for help, and they would find themselves quickly devoured by the beast that had assumed his form.

The door creaked softly as he pushed it open.

"Who's there?" the voice groaned from within.

Two words strung together. Could there be someone truly alive in here?

As he stepped through the second doorway and came fully into the room, the blue light illuminated a scene which he could have lived for many years without seeing, and have been perfectly happy about it. A man sat in a chair, and if the description had ended there, D'Arden would have been far more pleased.

The man – if he could still be called a man – was strapped down to the chair with heavy leather bands that wrapped around each wrist and the chair's arm. His head lolled back, and his guts had been opened as though with a vise. His innards lay strewn around the room, spread about him, and wrapped around his neck, and strung up and nailed to the ceiling in such a way that it looked like some sort of gruesome spider's web. There was blood everywhere. On the walls, on the floor, the man himself was covered in it almost from head to toe. D'Arden wondered just how it was that this poor creature was still alive, and then he noticed the trails of crimson light that crept up from the ground, infusing him with just enough manna to keep him from dying completely.

It was a truly gruesome scene of torture, and it had obviously been constructed very much on purpose.

The head lolled towards him, the eyes staring blankly as the man let out another groan. "Why can't I die? Why won't I die?"

"What happened here?" D'Arden whispered.

"They… they…" it started as what seemed almost a stutter, and then became a mantra as the man simply kept repeating the word over and over again.

It had happened already. The man's consciousness was lost. He still lived, but it was not a natural life, and what might had remained of his sanity was long fled this awful place. This grisly sight might have sat here for days, or even weeks, the poor wretch's life extended artificially through a careful application of the corrupted manna – leaving him not quite alive and not quite himself, but neither exactly dead.

"The horrors," the man whispered. For a brief moment, his eyes focused on D'Arden. "Save yourself!"

That's when D'Arden discovered just who 'they' were.

From all of the rooms of the house they suddenly came, the dead pouring out of the doorways as though they were the building's life blood suddenly released by the slicing of an artery. They groaned, they cried out, they shrieked with their still-taut throats. These were nothing like the rotted and desiccated corpses that he'd fought in the crypt. These were the bodies of the recently deceased, those driven out of their bodies by the corruption that pervaded every corner of this terrible place.

He cut at them with his sword, trying to drive them back. The walking dead staggered towards him, and though every one he cut down burst into the cobalt flames of the manna fire, it seemed as though a hundred more took their place. Where they had all come from he was not sure that he could ever know, and why they had all gathered here was a mystery that he doubted he would ever solve.

He stepped backward through the doorway, swinging his sword almost wildly as he went. They followed after him in a wave of stinking, rotting flesh and swinging limbs, desperately clawing at the air before them, staring ahead with unseeing, milky white eyes that twitched and danced in their skulls.

This was madness.

This was horror.

As he stumbled backwards out of the door that led

out to the sunlit streets, the dead immediately halted and began slowly retreating back into the house. Mikel stood, staring dumbfounded as he watched the corpses begin moving backwards in what seemed like one fluid motion.

"That's…"

"Sickening?" D'Arden asked sharply. "Horrifying? Going to haunt you for the rest of your days?" He shuddered, trying to shake off the image of the man inside, his innards strewn all over the room. "You have no idea."

"So that's what happened to all the people…" Mikel said slowly.

"Yes, that's where most of them are," D'Arden said. "My intuition tells me that not all of them are in that one house. There are probably more places like this where the corruption has spread so thickly that they congregate here. I would not be surprised to discover that there was a manna font sprung up inside that house. If I could burn the whole place down, I would."

He shook his head despairingly. "I don't know what I can do for them. There's too many of them in there for my sword arm to take care of it, and I'm not sure I have enough manna within me to destroy them all without recharging at least once. I could try, but it might well kill me."

"So what do we do?" Mikel asked.

"There's nothing we can do. Make sure none of your people come here after dark. I realize that you believe there might be someone left alive in here, but there is not. There is no one left in here that still needs your help. In fact, your captain should be closing this gate to ensure that none of these monsters get free and begin wreaking havoc on the rest of the city. Calessa Heights is lost, boy, and your family's home might well be next if we do not find this demon and destroy it!"

His harsh words and tone obviously frightened the boy, who took a few steps backwards from him. D'Arden didn't have time to care about the young soldier's fragile feelings. "The only reason that you and I are still alive right now is that the sun still shines on these streets. If night had already fallen, you and I would have been devoured by that horde of walking corpses."

"Can't we fight them? Put them out of their misery?" Mikel asked, his voice trembling slightly.

"If I had another Arbiter here with me, I might chance it," D'Arden said in a defeated tone. "Alone, there is no chance that I could destroy them all. I have not slept in two days, and I have already greatly overextended myself in the graveyard that your captain sent me to in order to gain access to the city's manna fonts. It is not possible for me to destroy them all myself, and your steel would be of little use but to slow them down a few steps."

He reached over his shoulder and slid the crystalline blade back home into its scabbard where it gave a satisfied click. He turned away from the house, trying to block out the sounds of the moaning dead that emanated now so loudly from within. "Calessa Heights is lost," D'Arden repeated. "I do not believe the demon is residing here. There is no one who would worship him here, no one left alive to venerate him and give him more power. This is not the place that we will encounter the demon, nor is it a place to make a pointless stand. Once I destroy the demon and purify the fonts, the corpses will collapse and then the houses can be cleaned out."

"Will anyone want to live here after something like

this?" Mikel said.

"I certainly would not," D'arden answered. "Come. We should report our findings to your Captain and have him impose an immediate full quarantine on this area. Now that we have disturbed the dead, if all entrances to this quarter are not closed off completely by nightfall, there will be many more dead in the morning.

"We should next check the font in the low quarter, where your family lives," he continued more softly. "If the corruption is not as strong there, it is a possibility that I may be able to purify that font and give myself a base of power to work from. If I can make myself stronger, it will make the demon weaker."

"You should rest before you do," Mikel said. "Two days is a long time to be awake."

"I have a room at the inn near the trader's gate," D'Arden said. "Perhaps you are right. It may be best to first take a repose and collect myself before attempting to purify a badly corrupted font on my own."

"Let's go see the captain," the boy said.

They hastily retreated from the high quarter.

**

"What do you mean it's lost?" Captain Mor demanded upon their return to the barracks.

D'Arden had been planning to break the news to the captain, but the boy had spoken up as soon as they entered. The Arbiter shook his head and spread his hands in defeat. "There is nothing that can be done. There is no one left alive in the Heights, Captain Mor. Not a soul that still lives... naturally," he amended, remembering the man

63

strapped to the chair in the house.

For a moment it appeared that Captain Mor would retort, to say something harsh and hostile and accuse D'Arden of giving up too easily, but then he simply collapsed into his chair, looking broken and wounded. "I cannot believe that it has gotten so far," he whispered. "How could this have happened?"

There were many things that D'Arden could have said, but few of them would have been properly diplomatic. Instead, he said carefully, "Mistakes have been made. A greater mistake may yet be made. You must immediately quarantine the Heights before any of the creatures in there are let loose in the city, and this must be accomplished before sundown today. Though they may have been lying dormant, they have now been awakened and will not wait long before seeking to feed."

Though he might have expected Mor to argue, the captain did no such thing. Instead, he merely nodded assent. "Very well. I'll have my men barricade off all of the gates to the Heights immediately. No one will go in or out from here on until this entire situation is resolved."

"Good then," D'Arden said with a small sigh. "If you'll excuse me, Captain, I will now take my leave so that I may rest. It has been a long few days and I seek the comfort of your inn."

"Was the boy a bother?" Mor said, jerking his thumb at Mikel.

"Not at all," D'Arden said graciously. "In fact, I would very much like it if you could spare him to accompany me on the next part of my investigation, once I awaken from my rest."

"Of course, master Arbiter," Mor said graciously.

"Anything that you require shall, of course, be yours."

So you would provide me, then, with an army of Arbiters to purify this gods-forsaken place? D'Arden thought inwardly, but said nothing.

"Thank you, Captain," he chose instead to say, and gave a slight bow. With only that, he turned and left the room, leaving Mikel and the captain behind him.

Once again on the streets of Calessa's trade quarter, he made his way up the short dead-end street and back to the main square where his inn lay. He approached the door and went inside, giving a curt wave to the publican, who gave him only a sharp nod of acknowledgement as he passed by.

Ascending the stairs both exhausted and energized with purpose, he crossed the long hallway to the room with the number on the door that matched the number etched into his key: thirty-seven. He turned the key in the lock and opened the door, revealing a small but serviceable room with a bed, table, two chairs, and a fireplace that lay cold but could quickly be revitalized with a few logs from the pile that sat beside it and a spark.

This is going to be far more difficult than I thought, he said to himself as he placed two pieces of wood on the fire and lit them with a wave of his hand. They came to life almost instantly, a merry blaze springing up and beginning to warm the icy chill that had pervaded the room, despite the bright sunlight outside.

He stripped off his gloves and rubbed his hands together before the flames to warm them. The insidious cold had even crept its way between the thick fabrics of his sword gloves, which had kept his hands warm through a driving snowstorm once, long ago, a much farther way north from here. Hunting evil in the snowbound tundra of the far northlands had been his first, and his least favorite, assignment as a fully named Arbiter. The cold here was indicative of more than just a long winter, and it would rob this place of the last sparks of life if left unchecked.

He did not intend to let anything like that happen.

Once the room had warmed to his liking, he sat on the sparse bed and crossed his legs before him. He did not need to sleep, only to wait for a few hours in a trance to refresh himself completely, and even less than that if he had a manna font nearby to draw from. The one that he had visited in the chapel a few blocks away was too far corrupted to draw upon, though, so he would have to rely on the earth itself to deliver his power to him.

D'Arden drew forth from its place on his belt the tiny, perfectly round, pointed and tapered blade that thrummed with a soft blue light, looking very much like a heartbeat. The heartblade pulsed in his hand with its energy, and he sighed. With only a moment's hesitation, he opened the front of his shirt and positioned the tiny blade just below the chest muscle on his left side. There was a tiny amount of pain as the perfectly sharpened instrument pierced his flesh and the muscle, and then just brushed the outside of his heart. He held his breath tightly, because any slight movement in the wrong direction could slice open his heart and send him to an early – and quite embarrassing – grave.

The hyper-concentrated manna within the heartblade released in a flash, and he felt the warmth and the ecstasy wash over him. He pulled the tiny dagger free from his flesh, and the wound healed as the blade exited, sealing immediately with the fresh power contained in the heartblade. It would recharge itself in time, though it might have more difficulty without direct access to a pure manna font. The heartblade was very important, and several failsafes had of course been written into its design. As the pain faded, he settled in for his regenerative trance.

He would have said a short prayer to the gods, but the last time he had seen someone do that, a magical gate had opened in midair, great beastly tentacles had reached through the opening and dragged the man through bodily, screaming and fighting and yelling and cursing the whole time. All those around him had simply averted their eyes, for they had known what was happening, and he had simply been left to stare, dumbfounded, watching as a man was snuffed out by those whose favor he sought.

It was not wise to speak to the gods.

III
THE LOW QUARTER

Images swirled around D'Arden's mind as the room faded away around him. His hands were placed securely on his knees, and though the thin mattress on the bed was softer than he was used to, he was able to find a comfortable enough position that allowed his consciousness to sink into trance.

As he did, he felt the corruption swell up around him, clawing at his consciousness, desperately seeking a way past his wall of purity and clarity. It wanted to get its claws into him, to drive him mad as it had done to the Arbiter who had preceded him here, to take away his sanity and drive him screaming into the catacombs beneath the city to vanish forever.

A thought haunted him that had crossed his mind briefly before; could it be that the source of the evil energy here was actually that Arbiter who had been here five years ago, and perhaps still was? Could it be not a demon at all, not a creature from another world, but a member of his own flock gone rogue? The thought troubled him deeply, to say the least, and it was with that thought on his mind that he descended fully into his healing and regenerative trance.

Normally he would perform his trance in the glow of a manna font, but he dared not do any such thing in this terrible place. Even the font in the graveyard had too much corruption for him to effectively draw any power from it. It was frightening and dangerous to be so cut off from the comforting source of his power, to have to reach far and away to replenish the manna that dwelled deep within him.

Reach though he did, sending his consciousness far across the land, trying to find the green grass and warm fields beyond the desolate landscape that surrounded Calessa. He longed to return to the high stone gates among the mountains that were home to the Arbiter's Tower, the place where he'd been raised, the place that he called home. There was a manna font seemingly on every corner there, always a place to draw their power from.

Finally he found himself able to connect to the land, just at the very edges of his spiritual reach. The corruption from Calessa was spreading, and if it was left entirely unchecked it would soon spread to the surrounding cities. If the demon's influence touched Aldur, a city nearly forty leagues to the north, the Arbiters might not have the forces to combat the demon at the height of its power.

He would not let that happen. He wished there was a way that he could contact his fellows, but there was no chance that the message would reach them in time. As always, they were spread to the far corners of the globe, searching out and destroying evil wherever it could be found. There were barely more than a handful of them now, plus a few in training at the Tower. Word would never reach them in time. It was up to him to destroy this evil and stop it in its tracks before it grew large enough to shake the foundations of the world itself.

D'Arden planted his spiritual feet upon the ground outside the range of the corruption, drinking up the sweet power of the land into himself, into his soul. It was sweet and cool and refreshing but also pleasantly warm in a way, making him feel as though he were home once again. There were only tiny traces, small inklings of the corruption in the manna that he drew inward.

For a few hours he sat outside the twisted land, reveling in the replenishment of his energy and a chance to truly rest. He'd expended much of his power in the mausoleum, fighting that dry corpse and the legions of its minions, and then expended yet more fighting against the undead in Calessa Heights. Although his power was nearly unlimited when he was near a pure manna font, without one nearby he became weak, and useless.

He hoped that there was still a chance to purify the manna font in the low quarter. The boy, Mikel, had said that the corruption was weaker there, that it hadn't yet spread to much of the populace. That alone was a hope, that he might be able to establish a foothold here in the city so that he might work outward to cleanse it of the danger.

When his strength had fully returned, he slowly drew his spirit back to his body. Carefully he returned to his flesh to ensure that he was not too quickly overwhelmed by the corruption during the transition back to the physical realm. The manna he had absorbed bolstered him though, heightened his strength both physical and mental so that when he returned to his body he no longer felt exhausted, drained and defeated; but instead energized and ready to face whatever dangers and trials lay ahead for him.

D'Arden opened his eyes once again. The fire he had lit in the fireplace had long since burned out, and the cold was creeping into the room again. A few weak embers glowed in the hearth, but the rest was cold, black ash. The room looked the same as it had when he had closed his eyes, but the slant of the sun was significantly lower, and the shadows in the room longer from the light streaming in the window.

It had been several hours at least, he mused. Slowly standing to ensure that nothing untoward had happened to his limbs while he'd been entranced, he made his way over to the window and looked at the sky. The position of the sun told him that it was well into afternoon, which was well enough. That would have given the captain and his men plenty of time to seal up the entrances to Calessa Heights, which would significantly reduce the danger to the rest of the population of the city.

He crossed the room and exited, making sure to the lock the door behind him. Slowly, he descended the staircase and entered the common room.

The patrons for the evening were beginning to trickle in, and there was a common sense of anxiety that seemed to pervade the room. As he crossed the threshold and entered the room fully, he saw a man clad in armor rise from his seat at a nearby table. It only took D'Arden a moment to realize that it was Mikel, the boy solider that had accompanied him to the Heights.

"Have you been here all afternoon?" D'Arden asked him as the young man came to greet him.

Mikel nodded. "The Captain said I should wait for you. He didn't want me to go off on a patrol and not be ready to go with you when you awakened."

D'Arden frowned slightly. He'd hoped that the Captain would at least send the boy back to the Heights, to ensure that the soldiers were blocking off the gates as he'd instructed. No matter, though – the fact that the boy was already here would save him a time-consuming search. He needed Mikel's expertise, since the boy had been born and raised in the low quarter.

"We should go," D'Arden said after a moment. "The longer we wait, the more the corruption will spread. If we are to have any hope of purifying the manna font in the low quarter, we must go there immediately."

"I'll lead the way," Mikel said. "We'll pass by my home on the way to the font chapel."

That would be fortuitous, D'Arden thought. The boy could visit his family while he attempted to purify the font. He suspected that there might be something there, a smaller danger that would be drawing the power of the font into itself, like there had been in the graveyard. That would prevent the corruption from becoming too concentrated there among the people, because something would be absorbing all of the power, similar to how he absorbed the pure manna from the earth.

It could not be the demon, he reasoned, for if the demon had taken up residence there the corruption would surely be stronger. The boy would have noticed at least some of his friends and neighbors acting strangely at least, and murderously mad at worst. If none of that had happened, perhaps there was a smaller presence, something that could be more easily dealt with. His only hope of saving Calessa lay with purifying one of the fonts in the city so that he could work outward from there, have a place to recharge, and also to have a way to locate where the demon was hiding.

He nodded to the boy, and together they left the inn. As he exited through the front door, D'Arden looked to the counter where the publican stood. As before, the publican merely gave him a curt wave with his grizzled hand, and D'Arden returned the gesture with an acknowledging nod.

The streets were lively in the afternoon in the trade quarter. Many people milled around, what must have been fully half of the remaining population of the city. They seemed remarkably unaffected by what lay beyond the gate into Calessa Heights; perhaps it was simply easier for them to put it out of their minds.

He followed Mikel among the merchant carts and through the crowds of people. The shouting, the yelling, the calling out of names and wares and prices was nearly deafening compared to the grisly silence he had experienced only hours earlier, and to the pleasant repose that had taken his attention since. In fact, he was quite surprised that his room in the inn had been so well insulated against the inundation of sound that lay outside.

They meandered their way along the streets and slowly the crowds of the trade quarter began to thin out. The streets began to look more desolate as the people began to be less and less frequent, and they passed through several neighborhoods which had obviously not been inhabited in some time.

"People are all congregating close to the trade quarter," Mikel said, as though he had read the Arbiter's mind. "The captain's got special provisions that allow folk to buy houses for people who died or had to be…" he swallowed hard, "…put down. They can buy 'em cheap, and it brings them in closer to where the rest of the people are, so they don't feel so lonesome. Sometimes the captain even lets them live there for free. Not like the owners care anymore, and people are so desperate to be a part of civilization that they don't mind living in the house of dead folk."

"A sad state of affairs indeed," D'Arden said.

"It's really only the trade folks who can afford the program, though," Mikel said. "You'll start to see more people again once we get close to the low quarter. There's all sorts of people in there who can't afford to move."

Mikel was right. As they wound their way through the streets and the buildings became less and less decorated, more worn and older-looking, D'Arden began to see the population pick up again. These were very different people than were found in the trade quarter. These people wore rags, many of them, and he began to feel conspicuous and out of place very rapidly. His road-worn travel clothes were like princely robes to these poor folk. It seemed that since the corruption had come to Calessa that their fortunes were growing more and more dire. They seemed happy enough, and D'Arden could not sense any large increase in corruption as they approached. Of course, the city was so thick with it that it was hard to distinguish one from the other, but this place did not have the oppressive ominous feeling that had pervaded the Heights. For all that they had little wealth, these people actually seemed to be genuinely happy.

"The font chapel is down this way," Mikel said, and D'Arden followed only a few steps behind him. It seemed strange to him what a sense of joy these people seemed to have in their lives, unaware that within the walls of their own city there lurked a danger which threatened to devour all of them: men, women and children alike.

D'Arden felt buoyed by the pure energy that he'd absorbed from the earth during his trance. Despite his knowledge of just how dire the situation was in this city, he could almost feel the genuine, warm joy that these people felt. It seemed to him as though purifying the manna font here in the low quarter would be little more effort than walking up to it. He felt invincible, alive, and ready to take on anything that would come his way.

If only that feeling could have lasted.

They approached the font chapel with some trepidation. D'Arden feared that it would be as badly corrupted as the one in the trade quarter, and that might well render his mission pointless. Mikel, of course, was simply worried about being exposed to the radiant power that lay within.

The font chapel was the nicest and most highly decorated building in the surrounding area. It was made of the cool white stone that all of the font chapels in this area were made from, while the rest of the buildings seemed to be made of rotting wood and thatch. It stood out like a red-tailed hart in an open green meadow.

As they stood before the door, D'Arden looked at the boy. "You should take this time to visit your family. They will have missed you, and you cannot enter the chapel with me. Go, now, and come find me in an hour. This may take some time as I do battle with the corruption on its own ground."

Mikel nodded and disappeared down one of the side streets, but not before handing D'Arden the key to the chapel's door. With a glance over each shoulder to ensure that there was no one within range of the energy's lethal light, he unlocked the door, pulled it open quickly, and stepped inside.

The corruption assaulted him immediately, but it was not as strong as the time before. There was some purity still left in the energy here, and it was enough, he thought, that he might be able to gain a foothold. As soon as he had closed the door behind him, he plunged his hands into the radiant light and stiffened with a cry of pain.

It was different here. Calessa was a huge city, and the high quarter was as far away from where he was currently as it could possibly be while still remaining within the walls of the city. While there was still corruption, and it was undeniable that it was growing and spreading, it did not seem to be wholly owned by the evil presence that made its home somewhere in the city. Instead, he could clearly feel that the manna was being drawn to a specific place, though he could not immediately tell where that place might be. This was more like the graveyard, then – some sort of lesser evil was directing the flow of the energy for its own gain. Control of this place had been relinquished by the demon to some minion, something dangerous in its own right, but perhaps not as deadly as facing down the evil that controlled this city.

This was something he could do. Despite the pain that the corrupted manna caused him, he felt elation at the thought. If he could locate this lesser evil and extinguish it, purify the spark of its evil and erase its very existence, he would have a foothold in the city. He could establish a base of operations here, in the low quarter, and branch outward in order to cleanse the whole city of its evil.

Withdrawing his hands from the pool of light he gave a quiet sigh. Now the question was only about locating whatever beast, whatever creature it was that was drawing the power from this font and corrupting it. He could find it.

Carefully, he secured the door to the font chapel behind him as he exited, to ensure that no one would accidentally let free the power that lay within. On the street, he paused to take a few deep breaths, to draw the manna out from inside himself. He closed his eyes and focused, trying to bring the trail of manna that would lead him to the danger to the forefront of his mind, to give his eyes the ability to see the flow of the manna as though it were an animal trail.

When once more he opened his eyes, it was there before him, clear as daylight. The trail wound through the streets, but it was a definite flow away from the chapel, going deeper into the low quarter. If Mikel were here, he could have been a better guide, but D'Arden did not want the boy involved in this any more than he needed to be. The young soldier would not stand a chance against a creature that could wield corrupted manna; he would be dead inside of a few seconds, and there would be little to nothing that D'Arden would be able to do to save him.

No, this would have to be his battle, and his battle alone. The steel of Mikel's sword might be helpful if whatever beast he was going to face might have living creatures that served it, but if the servants were touched by the corruption as well, there would need to be silver edges on that blade at least. It was better if he went in alone with his manna blade that would cut swaths through the enemy, a power that they would not be expecting, and take them fully by surprise.

**

He followed the manna trail through the streets of the low quarter, paying little attention to his route or direction. It was less important that he find his way back again, and more important that he locate the source of whatever it was that was siphoning the power from the nearby font.

After twisting and winding through the streets, taking sharp corners around buildings when the trail of manna went directly through them, and cutting through some abandoned barns, stables and other large buildings, he finally arrived at a door.

There was nothing special about this door; in fact, quite the opposite. The door was decrepit, almost collapsing inward under its own weight. It was rotten through and through, and there was nothing visible through the holes in the wood. It was all dark inside.

He regarded the door skeptically. Why would anything that could wield the power of the manna be hiding within a place such as this? It made little sense to him, but perhaps it was simply trying to hide, to control the power from a secretive place that no one would think to look, buried deep within the poorest section of the city.

It was impossible to deny, though, that this place was where the trail ended. It clearly went inside, and there was no denying that he felt the power growing here, collected beneath his feet. With a small sigh at the thought of once again having to go underground, he pushed open the rotten door and entered.

Immediately the sickly-sweet smell of decaying flesh assaulted his senses. Reeling from the intensity of it, he immediately pulled free his sword from its sheath on his back, and it came free with its characteristic rasp. The light immediately sprang to life, and he was suddenly able to see exactly why the atmosphere within the building was so terrible.

Bodies were piled around him in haphazard heaps,

flung atop one another. Some appeared as though they had perhaps been gnawed upon, others, which had obviously lain there for months undisturbed, had already begun rotting away. Some in-between, dead for maybe days or weeks, were swelled up to the point of bursting despite the horrific cold that would normally prevent such a thing from happening. All of the eyes of the corpses – not just some, but every single visible body that he could see – stared vacantly, blankly at whatever their head was turned towards. They were glassy, milky, and still freshly clear, but all of them simply stared, looking in every direction from where they lay, cast aside, upon the piles.

His stomach turned involuntarily, and he nearly dropped his sword as he stumbled backwards, trying to escape the terrible image. The cynical part of his mind, for a moment, thought: *At least they're dead, and not moving.*

Then another part of his mind chided him for cursing them like that, expecting the corpses to get up and begin moving at any moment.

They didn't.

In some ways, the blank-eyed staring was worse, he found as he tried to block his mind against the assault. At least if the corpses were moving he could destroy them, set the manna fire to them and watch them burn away in an instant. This, however, was far more unnerving as he stepped gingerly amongst the lifeless bodies, trying both to respect the dead and make his way past them. He used the light from his blade so that he would not tread on any of the corpses, but still managed to crack a lifeless finger here and there, wincing each and every time.

Evil was not enough to describe this sight. The corpses were dressed in rags, some of them barely covered, others lewdly exposing themselves to the darkened room with no further cares in the world. He gave a small shudder. This, to him, would be what hell was like: utter disrespect for the living, and the life force that he treasured so highly.

Finally he passed beyond the room with the piled corpses. Though the smell of rotten flesh was little better here, he also picked up on the scent of something else. Something animalistic, feral and dangerous was lurking here, below the city. It was not the demon that he sought, but rather – as he'd expected – something less, something dangerous but not all-encompassing. Something that was, perhaps, an enemy that could be faced and destroyed.

The room narrowed to a small corridor that continued further into the dank building. He could hear water dripping in the distance, falling from a fair height in tiny droplets, like a miniature waterfall. As he got further away from the corpses, the rooms began to smell less of corpse and more of mildew and wood rot. All he could see before him was darkness, relying on the azure light from his sword to indicate to him where the walls were and which direction they turned in.

Once again, he found his passage blocked by a door.

This door was more difficult to discern the features of, given the lack of light and the comparably small amount of detail revealed by the light of his manna blade. It appeared to be in somewhat better repair than the door outside, but he feared what might lay beyond it. Danger he was used to, and he was not afraid of a confrontation with a horrific fel beast, but down here in the dark amongst piles of corpses was the last place that he had ever wanted to find himself.

Gritting his teeth, he tried the handle on the door, only to find that it broke off in his hand. He muttered a curse under his breath and pushed gently on the door, but it steadfastly refused to budge even under a fair amount of pressure.

He decided to break it down.

Summoning the manna into himself to aid his body, he gave the door a mighty kick that might have rattled a steel gate. The wood gave under his strength, shattering inward with little more protest than a soggy, squishing sound as he reached the core. Fragments of the wooden door clattered down the stairs that were then revealed before him.

Once again his stealth had been broken. It was almost as if these creatures knew that he was coming long in advance and had prepared for the eventuality, putting up barriers between themselves and him so that they would be properly warned of his entrance.

That was ludicrous, of course.

Cautiously, so as not to step on a soggy piece of wood and end up tumbling headfirst down the flight of stairs, for he knew not how far into the darkness below that they would extend, he began to descend the stairs. After several steps he reached a landing, and found that they continued downward a few feet away.

Halfway down, the steps turned from wood to stone, and still, they continued downward.

When he had touched on several landings and still the stairs continued down, he began to wonder just how far into the earth this cellar went.

Finally, when he came at last to ground once again, he looked around and could find no further stairs continuing downward. He looked up, back the way he had come, and of course there was no light at the top of the stairs to indicate how far he might have descended into the earth. If he'd had to guess he must have been sixty feet below ground level, but he had never heard of such a cellar being dug before, and certainly not in the low quarter of Calessa.

This, then, must be a passage to some kind of ancient ruin, he thought to himself. He wondered if the citizenry of Calessa were even aware of this staircase. It crossed his mind to wonder who had built such a massively deep cleft into the earth, and whether or not he should be concerned about its denizens.

The manna trail had clearly led him down the stairs, down here into the earth, but he had no idea which direction to begin moving in. The darkness was chokingly thick here, closing in around him and making him feel claustrophobic, although there were no walls nearby that he could detect. The thick smell of dust filled his nostrils, but he was mostly glad to be rid of the scent of mildew and rotten flesh. It seemed to him as though perhaps no one had been down here in centuries, but he knew that would not be the case, as some evil was lurking down here, waiting for something... although he knew not what, exactly, it would be waiting for.

He held his sword aloft, trying to get his bearings. The staircase seemed to touch down in the middle of a large room, and in no direction did the blue light reflect off of any structures except the staircase itself.

A red glow caught his attention out of the corner of his eye. He whirled to face it, and suddenly realized that he had been lured into a trap.

He could now see the walls, reflecting the glow of the beast that lurked down here. As the glow brightened, it revealed a shape that was not unlike that of a wolf, but larger, stronger, more deadly. Its eyes gleamed brightly with that same dull, angry crimson light that seemed so common in the enemies that he faced, all driven by hatred, anger and corruption to become the evils that they were.

It took a few steps toward him, releasing off puffs of corrupted manna fire as each humongous paw touched the ground. D'Arden took one step back, and then another, and the creature continued its forward stride, closing the gap with each foot it set forward. It bared long, white teeth that gleamed violet in the combined light from them.

"So, the Arbiter has come to visit," the creature slavered. "I've been waiting for you to find my lair."

As it came further into the light, D'Arden felt his blood run cold. The thing was three times the size of a normal wolf, and its fur was a thick charcoal black, looking as though it had been set on fire several times, and in fact, it still reeked of burnt hair. It began to circle around to his right and the Arbiter sidestepped, making sure that his sword remained between him and the beast.

"What do you mean you've been waiting for me?" D'Arden asked, hoping to keep the beast distracted while he studied it, looking for some sign of weakness that he might be able to exploit. His initial once-over did not reveal anything promising. "How could you have possibly known that I was here?"

The beast laughed, a grating, rumbling sound that was only barely recognizable as such – anyone less versed in the ways of the fel beasts would have simply taken it as a warning growl. "Good try, Arbiter. You won't fool me that easily. My master would not take it lightly were I to divulge his secrets."

"So you admit to me that you're not the master here?"

D'Arden said, intentionally bear-baiting the beast. "You admit that you're still little more than the forest creature you once were, but now domesticated and good only for lapping at your master's feet and chasing bones like some dog?"

The fel wolf started to growl, but it caught in the creature's throat and turned into a chuckle. "I see your game, Arbiter. I am not simply a beast that can be prodded and goaded into a mindless and thoughtless attack. I am more than what I came from."

"I'm not sure I see it," D'Arden said, still circling around the creature as it attempted to circle him. "I think you can be provoked just like any other beast of your nature can."

"Try me, Arbiter," the beast said with a hideous grin.

Without breaking his circling stride, D'Arden summoned up some of the manna he'd stored during his trance and focused it into his off-hand. A blue fireball began to build there in his palm, lighting up the room more fully. It grew until it was a blinding white, brilliant focus of purified manna energy that snapped and crackled exactly like real fire, except that no sound issued forth from it at all.

"An impressive display," the fel wolf growled. "Dare you use so much of your power all at once, Arbiter? I think it would weaken you too far, and if you missed, could you still fend off my assault?"

"Even the splash of this pure energy would weaken you," D'Arden spat back at him, the light from the manna fire-ball pleasantly warm against his skin. "I believe that we would be on equal footing afterwards."

The beast snorted. "You know so little, Arbiter. You

speak of purity, and yet you have no idea what purity is. Are your stuffy morals and defense of the weak really pure, Arbiter? In my eyes, power is pure. Unfettered, wholesome power that knows no boundaries and no limitations. Power that you could have yourself, Arbiter, if only you would let go of your petty morals and sense of justice."

D'Arden rolled his eyes, almost losing his concentration on his manna fire-ball. "Really?" he asked. "You, a corrupted and twisted thing that barely resembles its lupine parents for its descent into decay and madness, dare to lecture me on such things? You dare to try and tempt me away from my path? The very thought is ludicrous!"

"Not so ludicrous after all!" the beast roared as it leapt at him through the air.

D'Arden was nearly taken off-guard by its assault, for which he cursed himself inwardly. He had been trying to catch the beast off its guard, but instead he found that he was the one caught. Although his concentration on his manna attack had waned slightly, still he brought his left hand forward in a powerful, open-handed strike motion, throwing the collection of manna at the oncoming beast.

It exploded against the fur with a flash of white light and a sound like thunder echoing in the stone chamber far beneath the earth. The beast was caught fully in the chest by the blast and flung backwards, its forward momentum completely reversed by his powerful counterattack. The fel wolf flew backwards with a howl and slammed against the far wall.

D'Arden watched with satisfaction as the manna flames began to devour the beast.

His satisfaction quickly died as the beast stood up and

shook off the cobalt flames, the red glow in its eyes not dimmed in the slightest. D'Arden found his resolve shaken slightly; the beast had weathered a strong blow – not his strongest, certainly, but dangerous nonetheless – without so much as flinching.

"I hope that was not your best effort, Arbiter," the wolf said with a feral grin. "It was good, but I am stronger than that. My master has given me great power in this place, and has promised me an endless supply of food once he controls the whole city without reservation."

D'Arden cocked his head slightly. "So all of those bodies up there… those are your food? But you've hardly touched them."

"I no longer hunger for flesh, Arbiter. I have little taste for the stuff. My master has granted me the power to live only on the purest sustenance – raw human blood. I take what I need, and I leave the rest for the crows."

"Except the crows can't get to them if they're lying around inside," D'Arden said, almost jovially. "So why don't you leave them outside? Don't you have free run of the city at night, to do as you please and strike terror into the populace? For all of the people who are dead up there, hundreds more are in the streets right now as we speak, laughing and going about their lives, just like always. They do not fear you."

"They will," the wolf growled. "I will make sure that they do."

"Yes, perhaps," D'Arden said. "But when?"

The wolf leapt at him again, but this was not the same timed strike that it had executed previously. This was more instinctive, reaching out with its snapping jaws and a rumbling growl that turned into a harsh bark. D'Arden rolled under it as he saw it coming and drew the manna blade along the beast's belly. The wolf gave a cry of agony and came to its feet a few yards away, and the Arbiter rolled to his feet with a look of triumph on his face.

The wolf was bleeding heavily now, its body nearly gushing in some places that same thick, luminescent fluid that had come from the fel dogs outside the city, and the manna fire was eating away at the blood, seeking to purify the corruption within. The blue flames crept up the trailing fluid, but never seemed to quite reach the fur. It was obviously resisting the purification, but it had been weakened – D'Arden could see that in its eyes.

"So, have you had enough yet?" D'Arden asked with a glint of the manna fire in his eyes. "Do you really want to push this any farther? Give up now and I may let you return to the forest and your cursed brethren there, two of which I slew before I entered this godforsaken city, and another that I will slay now before either one of us leaves here!"

The wolf panted, but still managed to laugh. "You have nowhere to run, Arbiter, and nowhere to hide. This is my lair, and you will die here as surely as you would die if you were to face my master. You must be weakening; there is no chance that you could have found a source of pure manna anywhere near this city. Everything you touched would have only weakened you further, and now I will do the same!"

D'Arden worked hard to hide the smile that sprang to his lips. The wolf had underestimated him and his ability to reach out spiritually for the manna – it thought that he was exhausted.

The wolf's arrogance would be its downfall.

The Arbiter charged forward and swung his sword in a cutting arc. The wolf leapt aside and came back around swiftly, its jaws closing on the air that D'Arden had been standing in only seconds before. D'Arden used the force from his twisting aside to bring his sword downward in a cleaving strike that would have severed the wolf in half had he caught flesh. Instead, his sword only cleft fur, sending strands of hair floating down to the floor.

The fel wolf, whose wounds had healed now, made a wheezing noise which was even more like a laugh than the previous growl. "Do you really believe that you stand a chance against me, Arbiter? Do you really think that you can defeat me in your weakened state? I am going to tear open your throat and drink every last drop of sweet, manna-touched blood from your body, and then leave your corpse for the crows along with the rest of the sorry folk above!"

D'Arden lowered himself into a crouch, holding the sword threateningly between the two of them. He allowed a hint of the smile he had suppressed earlier to touch his lips. "Would you believe me, beast, if I told you that you had underestimated my power?"

The wolf's jaws hung open and it made the wheezing laughter sound again. "I would say that you were simply trying to delay me to find an opportune moment to strike me and catch me off my guard."

The element of surprise was his only chance. D'Arden willed up as much manna from his veins as he could possibly muster, but did not allow it to show anywhere outside his body. His eyes might have glowed slightly brighter, but the wolf would never notice in the light of his manna blade. "You have underestimated me," he said, allowing the small smile to spread into a full grin.

"Die, Arbiter!" the wolf cried, leaping once more into the air.

Thrusting out his hand in the same motion as before, his palm turned outward and his fingers kept close together, he summoned up all of the energy that he could possibly muster into that single point and compressed it, held it so tightly that he felt as though for a moment he might simply explode into nothingness, and then suddenly relaxed his concentration and allowed it to flow forth.

Any normal man would have been blinded by the explosion of manna that emitted from D'Arden's outstretched hand. The light flared brighter than the sun itself for an instant, a single moment in time and then rocketed outward with the force of a lightning strike. It almost appeared to be liquid as it struck outward, catching the wolf full in the chest and crackling around it, the sound of thunder echoing in the deep stone chamber. The wolf let out a yelp that was nearly as loud as the thunder itself, its voice amplified by the corruption that dwelled within it, and the resulting cacophony ached deep in D'Arden's ears.

The wolf was slammed back against the wall as before, but this time, it seemed that D'Arden could feel the very foundation of the building shake with the force. Stone was chipped and knocked loose from the wall, falling to the floor in bits and powder. Dust was dislodged from the ceiling dozens of feet above them, and sand trickled down into the chamber.

The manna fire was licking at the wolf's fur now, and the russet glow that the fel beast sported had dimmed considerably. The blue flames were consuming bits of the wolf's fur and flesh near its feet and around its face. It let out a deep, rumbling growl, but even its summoning of power could do little against the force that D'Arden had unleashed upon it.

"No," the wolf snarled. "No! How? How did you…"

D'Arden took a step forward, the light shining from his manna blade still as bright as a moment before as he reabsorbed some of the energy that had splashed off of the wolf and returned to the earth. He approached the wolf with confidence, knowing that his enemy had been weakened by the surprise assault.

"As I said, beast… you underestimate me," D'Arden said grimly. "You believed that because you have power here that you were the stronger of us, so instead of fighting cautiously, you fought with too much confidence. For that is your undoing, beast… your instincts have not yet gone enough to think that you might, for once, be at a disadvantage when fighting a mere man."

With those words, D'Arden lunged forward and thrust the blade deep between the fel wolf's ribs. The beast let out a howl and tried to snap its jaws at the Arbiter's arms, but D'Arden brought up one of his thick-soled boots across its snout sharply, and snapped its head back to the side. Once the manna fire had penetrated its thick outer skin, the wolf simply could resist the purification no longer. It gave a long, mournful death howl that echoed around him as the pure manna drove deep within its twisted heart and began to unmake the wolf from the inside out, driving out the corruption that gave it the dangerous and evil intelligence and returning its flesh to the power of the land.

Finally, the fel wolf's muscles relaxed and it fell

lifelessly to the stone floor. It was then that the manna flames began in earnest, lapping at the corrupted flesh and fur and bone, blazing brightly and eagerly and turning into a veritable azure bonfire. D'Arden took a few steps back, allowing the manna flames to run their course and ensuring that he did not himself get caught up in the blaze. What power was thrown off in the consumption he drew back into himself to replenish his own reserves.

Finally, when the azure flames had died and the wolf was no more, D'Arden turned himself back to the stone staircase. There was nothing left here now in this ancient stone cellar beneath the city.

He found himself exhausted, his body and mind drained from the incredible assault that he had just undergone. Each stair that he climbed was burning agony in his limbs, and he felt several times heavier than he was. As he reached each landing he would stop for several seconds and take deep breaths, careful not to draw in too much breath that would overwhelm him but also finding himself gasping for the sweet cool air. He could sense that he was nearing the top of the staircase as the smell of rot began to grow in his nostrils once more.

Finally he reached the top of the stairs, back into the rotten and mildewed wooden building at the ground level. The only thing that drove him forward, knowing that he would have to pass once more through the disturbing chamber piled with the bodies of the dead, was the thought that he could once again return to the font here and purify it of its evil, and absorb the power into himself so that not only could he recharge, but he could set himself up here, rather than in the horribly corrupted trade center where he roomed currently, and begin planning a strategy that would help him in saving this city from the depths that it had plunged to.

It was his purpose, he reminded himself, even though as he passed through the ranks of the staring-eyed dead that he briefly considered joining them himself in death from exhaustion. This was the greatest undertaking of his existence, to determine why this place had gotten so far, and what was driving the corruption to reach further and further outward as though it intended to devour the entire world.

Finally, he stumbled back out through the wooden door that led to the street and slammed it behind him, rattling the panes in the shattered out windows of the building that he stood beneath. The sun seemed impossibly bright after the session he had spent deep beneath the earth. He squinted his eyes and still they were overwhelmed by the brightness, and he was forced to squeeze them closed as he drew in breath after breath of fresh air at last, though the cold burned his lips, his tongue and his chest as he gasped as though he were a fish pulled from its pond.

After some time, he found that he was able to open his eyes again without immediately being forced to close them again. The sun still seemed too bright, and the colors of the world seemed strange and distant to him, but he knew that those would return in time. Once he could see his feet and the cobblestones before him again, he began to make his way back through the streets of the low quarter, trying to recall his path from before without becoming too lost.

Despite his best efforts, he sound found that he was hopelessly lost in the mazelike streets of the city. He recognized no landmarks, and he had been too intent on his path previously to leave a trail of crumbs or markings for himself. He could not find a single person on the streets – they had apparently all come together in a single area to huddle together in these miserable times, for which he could not blame them, but it did make it difficult to ask for directions.

Simply collapsing would have, quite literally, gotten him nowhere, so rather than give up and sit on an abandoned step he continued to wander, half in a blinded haze, through the streets, simply hoping that he might come upon the font chapel or a single building that he recognized.

At last, his salvation came on the wind.

"Master Arbiter!" called out a familiar voice. The boy. Mikel.

"Here!" D'Arden croaked, and it seemed to him that his voice belonged to someone else entirely. "I'm here!"

Footsteps approaching. Sensing that there was finally another human being nearby, D'Arden collapsed onto one knee. That strike to take down the fel wolf had drained him more than he realized, and he felt his head spinning about him. The darkness was once again closing in on him, but this was not the oppressive darkness that had surrounded him in the cellar, but instead a comforting, warm blackness that offered him solace in its embrace.

"Master Arbiter!" the boy's voice said again. He was nearby now, rushing to D'Arden's side. He felt a warm hand on his shoulder and fought to stay conscious. Another hand supported him, kept him from simply falling into the dust to lie there.

With that strength beside him to bolster him,

D'Arden fought back the unconsciousness that threatened to engulf him. Slowly his vision returned, and he looked into the concerned eyes of the young soldier that had led him here, to the place of his first real victory in this impossible fight.

"Thank you," D'Arden gasped. "You found me."

"It's been hours," Mikel said. "I came back to the font chapel, just like you said, but you weren't there. What happened?"

"I found the source of the corruption here," D'Arden said. "It was all centered in a selfish wolf, that should have been using the power to expand his influence, but instead all he cared about was drawing inward and building his power, luring his victims to him and holing up within the earth. His mistakes are our triumph, Mikel. The wolf is gone, defeated by its own base instincts, and we can now purify the font here in the low quarter." He paused for a moment and looked around them. "Where are we?"

Mikel pointed along the road to an ancient stone gate that was crumbling and nearly fallen inward. "That's the Old City, down that road there. Nobody's lived there for decades. It's all abandoned now, ever since they built the new city here. You're by Calessa's south gate."

He had wandered far then, D'Arden supposed. He reached out, and the boy grasped his hand firmly, helping him get to his feet. Though he still felt dizzy, he no longer felt as though he might collapse at a moment's notice. The thought of victory drove him onward now.

"We must go back to the font chapel near your home," D'Arden said. "Lead me there, Mikel. We must get there immediately."

The boy nodded, not questioning the urgency in his

tone for a moment. D'Arden could not follow a single one of the turns they made through the streets, but Mikel seemed to know every side alley and every street as though they belonged to him. Having grown up in this part of the city, he reflected, the boy probably had played in these streets as a child, which would of course explain why he knew them so well.

After what seemed like an eternity, they arrived before the door of the font chapel once more. D'Arden stared at it as though it were his sole salvation. This was his chance, his only chance, and it was a slim one. It had already been some time since he'd defeated the wolf down in the chamber beneath the earth. It was only a matter of time before the demon realized that his minion was gone and no longer siphoning power from this font, and sent in something to clean up the mess.

"Stand back, lad," D'Arden said, waving one hand at the boy. Mikel dutifully backed up several paces. "Now, don't come following me, no matter what you hear in there, do you understand?"

"I understand," Mikel said.

"Good," the Arbiter said. He brought the key out of his pocket and once more unlocked the heavy door that kept the radiant energy within. As quickly as possible, he opened the door, stepped inside, and closed it behind him.

There was still corruption flowing in the manna here, but he could feel that its influence had faded. The demon that lived here in Calessa had obviously been counting on its lupine minion to take control of this area and its power, but instead the wolf had lingered in its lair, merely taking what it needed in order to survive and build its power. It was a fatal mistake that he could not afford to repeat; once he had built up his power here just enough, he would need to make his next move quickly in order to catch the enemy as unaware as possible.

Once more he plunged his hands into the pool of light, and stiffened. The power surging through him, combined with his exhaustion, was almost more than he could bear. He had used a lot of energy defeating the fel wolf, and now purifying the font was nearly too much for him. He felt the pull of the manna tug at his soul, at his flesh, persuading him to join it and give up his life to become one with the earth. He fought against that urge, resisted its siren call. Instead he flooded the font with what pure energy remained from his trance, pouring all of it into the river in the hopes that what he carried within him would be enough to cleanse the font fully, so that he might then immediately begin drawing power from it to sustain himself.

It was agony; the tug on his soul became nearly too much to resist. He cried out in pain, in ecstasy, they blended together and his mind began to meld with the earth and become one with the flow and he could feel the power shining out of his eyes...

The heavy thunk behind him of the door opening snapped him back to consciousness. He heard the squealing of the hinges behind him, and he turned around to face whatever new threat had come to him, now interrupting this most crucial work. He drew his sword off his back...

He came face-to-face with the wide-eyed stare of the young soldier.

"Master Arbiter, I..." the boy stiffened immediately. The power was still radiating from D'Arden, so strong he thought it must be shining through his very flesh. Mikel cried out in pain and collapsed to the ground as the energy washed over him. He began screaming, sobbing as the light from the manna began to twist his flesh.

"Why?" D'Arden asked, his voice echoing like thunder.

"I..." the boy screamed again as he tried to speak, and D'Arden could see the flesh beginning to melt from his face. "I came to warn you! Some... something is coming!"

"YOU SHOULD HAVE STAYED AWAY!" D'Arden roared, awash in anguish and rage and confusion and loss, for he knew already that the boy was doomed.

With no choice but to leave the boy to his hideous fate, D'Arden turned back to the pool of manna, plunging his hands deep within it again even as he dropped his sword to the floor. The shrieks of the boy faded rapidly to piteous wailing, and then merely to moans as the manna forcefully drew out his soul and transformed his flesh, likely into something truly hideous. Exposure to the light of the manna would reveal the worst in a normal man, destroy the façade of normal humanity and bring forth the truth from them in the most painful manner possible.

As the flow of manna within the font shifted from corruption to purity, D'Arden felt the energy immediately flow into him. He felt rejuvenated, his mind snapped back to full alertness. Now that the balance of power within the font had tipped in his direction, he could draw his power from it. He felt elated, the joy surging through him as surely as the power itself did.

He withdrew his hands at last when he felt as though he was brimming with so much of the manna energy that he felt radiant and nearly invincible. It was only then that he remembered the plight of the poor soul, laying on the ground behind him, completely destroyed by the energy that sustained him.

D'Arden turned, expecting to see some horrifying vision lying on the ground just outside the door of the font chapel. He had seen many men in his time that had been struck by the light of the manna font, most of whom had turned into something resembling a creature out of a child's nightmare or campfire ghost story. They usually ended up with their limbs twisted about, looking as though they had broken themselves several times in an attempt to get away from the horrid things that were happening to them.

Despite his desperate hope, there was no solace to be found here.

The boy's innocent form had become twisted into a frightening monstrosity, its flesh blackened and withered. As he watched, it scrabbled to its feet, sporting long claws that had sprouted unceremoniously from its hands. Only a few strands of wiry hair remained of the boy's shock of brown, and those strands stood out straight from the creature's head. The boy's clothes had sloughed off the creature's greatly reduced mass, and the beast stood naked before him, though nothing remained that would define it as indecent. It entirely ignored the soldier's blade on the ground between them, and instead it stared at him with yellow eyes that burned with hunger. Mikel had not been exposed to the light of the manna font long enough to die, it seemed… but only long enough to awaken.

The fel beast let out a shriek, a cry of both pain and hunger.

It lowered its head and rushed at him.

Sorrowfully, D'Arden simply stepped aside. The boy's lack of experience in the matter of fighting even showed through to this hungry monster that he'd become. In a single motion, D'Arden drew the crystalline blade from the scabbard on his back and cleaved downward, splitting the beast in twain at the waist.

The creature that was once Mikel tumbled to the ground in two halves, each one quickly dissolved by the blue purifying flames.

D'Arden stood in the silent streets for a moment, his head bowed.

Then, in his ears rang the boy's warning, as clear as though he'd said it that same moment. *Something is coming.*

He slid the manna blade back into its sheath and stepped outside the chapel, slamming the door closed behind him. He looked to the left and to the right, but he could neither see nor hear anything approaching. What had the boy seen or heard, then, that had bothered him enough to make him enter the chapel?

The sun had set over the horizon only a few minutes before, and darkness was beginning to settle in. As he stood there in the cold with a breeze blowing across him, he heard a scuttling sound, and then a chattering in some language that he could not decipher, though it sounded ancient and stilted like a philosopher's tongue.

The sound was rapidly retreating in the direction from which he and Mikel had come a few minutes before. He stared in that direction, knowing that less than a mile away stood the gate to the Old City.

That, then, was his next destination. Whatever it was that was scrabbling across the cobblestones was unmistakably heading in that direction, and though it could potentially be a distraction – some minion sent by the demon to lead him down the wrong path and away from his lair – it could also be something important, exactly the direction that he needed to be going.

He had no other leads, and his only guide to the city was dead. The font here was purified, and he knew that if he waited too long, the demon's forces would come to reclaim it.

D'Arden looked toward the font chapel where Mikel had fallen, refusing to lay eyes on where the fel beast that had replaced him had died. He had seen too many things like this in his short lifetime, too many innocent lives stolen away by the power he served, and the corruption against which he fought. His dark hair streamed outward in a soft breeze that passed, and his black cloak flared outward, casting a dark shadow across the door of the chapel.

Wasted life was an incredible shame.

Shaking his head slowly, the Arbiter set off down the street.

IV
THE OLD CITY

D'Arden recalled the streets with more clarity this time as he walked along them with purpose. The sun had set beyond the horizon only a few minutes before, and already stars were beginning to appear in the cold night sky. The Deadmoon was rising over the trees to the east, as it did every night, and though it now appeared as a haunting orange in the sky, soon it would bathe the landscape in its pale bone-white glow, draining the color from everything and rendering the world in shades of gray.

Even in the dim light of the setting sun and the rising moon, D'Arden found that he remembered the way through the streets, back along the route they had come when retreating from the ancient gate that led to the Old City. Calessa was one of the oldest cities in the land, having been founded nearly a thousand years before on the site of a river. When that river dried up, the harbor and docks had been abandoned and most of the population moved into the denser part of the city. Eventually, what came to be called the Old City was entirely abandoned, sitting alone and desolate by the side of a dry river.

History was one of the subjects they were required to study most strongly during the strenuous training to become an Arbiter, and he knew the history of most of the cities and towns and lands nearby as well as he knew his own life. With the ability to use the manna freely within the tower, they had been able to call up images of the past and see it as though through a window, watching battles and the rise and fall of kingdoms and knights and the Arbiters themselves, as though it had been somehow recorded in moving pictures. In fact, it had been recorded, in a way – every event left an imprint in the flow of the manna beneath and throughout the land, so that every happening was remembered by the world itself.

Once more he stood before the old, crumbling gate of Old Calessa. He frowned; the scent of the corruption, the feeling of a concentration of power was strong beyond that gate. Though on this side he could feel the manna flowing freely, pure and vibrant, he somehow knew that one step beyond that forgotten gate would land him squarely in unfriendly territory once more.

The demon had done many terrible things to this place, but D'Arden had trouble imagining what horrors might be lurking amongst the moss-covered, crumbling stones of Old Calessa.

The sounds of battle reached his ears; strange sounds indeed for such a cold and desolate night. With one hand he drew the crystalline manna blade from the sheath on his back, and it came free with a low rasp. The cerulean light emitted forth in a gentle glow, forcibly adding color to the rapidly fading colors of the world around him.

He took a few steps towards the gate. The sounds of battle were unmistakable; steel on steel. He was almost certain he heard arrows flying through the air and hitting against something solid, possibly stone. Holding the sword parallel to the ground, he broke into a dead run through the gate, only flinching slightly as he crossed the threshold separating his power from the enemy's.

D'Arden skidded to a halt at the intersection of what had once been two roads, with the buildings crumbled around him, a few of them showing their foundations through large holes in the walls. Directly ahead of him were two soldiers, dressed in full armor, crouched behind rubble as arrows broke against their cover. They had no ranged weapons of their own. Up ahead he could hear the sound of ringing steel clearly in the darkened evening.

One of the soldiers pulled what looked like a knife out of a hidden holster within his boot, and stood up, perhaps to throw it at the enemy. Instead, an arrow pierced his throat. Gagging, the soldier stumbled backwards, clutching at the bladed shaft with his hands while blood streamed down over his silvery armor and stained it bright red. Choking, gasping, he collapsed to the ground and shortly expired.

The other soldier looked back in his direction, and surprise registered on her face. "Who are you?" she demanded, as another arrow snapped and shattered into many small pieces on the stones around them.

"My name is D'Arden Tal," he answered. "I am an Arbiter."

The soldier shut her eyes tightly as a gasp came from the road up ahead. It was followed shortly by a guttural male scream, the sound a man makes as his innards are unexpectedly released by the point – or the blade – of a sword.

"That's it… I'm the last one," she whispered. "I'm going to die."

D'Arden began boldly striding forward. He had no idea what it was that lay beyond those rocks, and he had no inkling as to what it might be that had managed to slay at least these two soldiers in such a short amount of time with such deadly accuracy. If they were using steel, they could not be touched too deeply by the corruption

– elsewise they would simply be using their ill-gotten manna gifts.

As he passed the rubble that the soldier was using for cover, they came into view. They were about his height, but they had dusky, leathery red-grey skin that covered their entire bodies. Protrusions of bone stuck out from their heads and their backs, and great tusks adorned their broken faces. These were *zagoths*, related to true demons, but not the dangerous, corruption-spreading kind. These demons were simple warriors, minions perhaps of the greater demon that dwelled within the city, but perhaps not. These creatures plagued the landscape, raiding cities and slaughtering neither for food nor sustenance, but purely for the joy of killing. They thrived off it, requiring nothing else to fuel them and drive them onward for more killing. They were disgusting things, but they were sharply intelligent and their dark eyes glittered with malevolence.

Two of them nocked arrows in their bows, both of which were likely made of human bones. The arrows flew at him, and the world itself seemed to slow down.

His manna blade flashed cobalt in the night air as he swung it once and then again in rapid succession before him. Each arrow shattered as the sword cut through it, the bladed tips knocked harmlessly away. Not breaking his stride, he took three more steps forward and cut down sharply at the *zagoth* holding a curved and serrated steel blade, standing over the body of the third soldier. It turned to face him, but not in time. The manna sword cut through the flesh and bone of the shoulder, and the demon let out a howl that echoed amongst the crumbling buildings. Blood came forth, not the red blood of a human wound, but instead the thick, black ooze that flowed through the bodies of the dark ones that walked the land. The manna fire could not take hold in these demons, for they did not rely on the corrupted manna for their power. There was nothing to be purified here – these creatures, such as they were, were natural.

The sword was his only weapon here – collected blasts of manna worked well against demons and those touched by the corruption, but they could do little against the pure and the natural. So, rather than rely on the manna fire to dissolve the *zagoth* that now shrieked in agony before him, he brought his sword around for another swing that separated the demon's head from its shoulders in a flash of light.

He spun gracefully around, having heard two more arrows leave the strings of the bone bows. The sword followed his movements, neatly deflecting two more arrows and shattering their shafts into hundreds of tiny shards. With a cry, he charged forward as one of them attempted to load another arrow, but it never came out of the quiver. D'Arden's blade whistled through the air and cut through the *zagoth*'s left arm and deep into the chest cavity, causing the black ooze to spout forth and the demon to groan and collapse into the dirt.

Just one aggressor left. He heard the next arrow coming, but he did not have time to spin and deflect it with his sword. It sank deep into the side of his thigh as he came around, and he cried out in pain as the metal pierced flesh and rent muscle in its path. Blood began to flow down his right leg as he rushed forward, too lost in the battle for the arrow to do much to slow his momentum. As the manna blade came around at the last demon, it attempted to hold up its bow to deflect the incoming attack. The bone was too brittle, and it shattered even as the blade cut into the crown of the *zagoth*'s head, separating a good three inches of skull off above its eyes. There was a spray of dark, pitch-like blood that splattered against the walls of the nearby stone foundations, and then all was silent.

As the adrenaline faded from his veins, D'Arden felt the pain of the arrow in his leg very sharply. He cried out once more and sagged heavily against the closest stone wall, closing his eyes and breathing deeply to regain his balance. The world swam around him. He only hoped – he did not pray, for to pray was to die – that the arrows had not carried any kind of poison on their tips. A flesh wound he could live with, and might even be able to seal long enough for him to finish his mission without too much undue scarring, but he would not be able to deal with a poisoned arrow. A toxin would overcome him in minutes, as his body was weakened against attacks which bore no trace of manna, but simply natural danger.

Gripping the arrow shaft tightly in one hand, he snapped it off. He closed his eyes tightly and groaned against the agony as the arrow moved and blood flowed out more strongly. Holding what remained of the shaft as tightly as possible, though it was slick with blood, he pulled hard on it and it came free with little additional damage. The arrow was not bladed nor was it barbed, but a simple round point designed for a pinpoint, killing shot. These *zagoths* had known that they would be fighting soldiers.

They hadn't counted on an Arbiter.

He turned back to where the soldier was still hiding behind the rubble. He saw her face appear from behind the rocks, and then, as she sensed that the danger had passed, she emerged from her cover.

"How did you do that?" she asked.

He slid his manna blade home into its sheath that hung from his back, and it clicked as it locked into place. "Practice."

She looked down at the wound on his leg. "You're bleeding."

"It will pass," he grunted, the pain of the wound still very fresh and at the forefront of his mind. "I'll be fine. It wasn't deep nor was it crippling. I was very glad to determine that the arrows weren't poisoned."

He looked into her eyes – the black pupils at the center were taking up most of the colored part of both eyes. She was obviously suffering from some kind of battle shock, most likely from seeing two of her compatriots coldly dispatched.

"Where did these *zagoths* come from?" he asked, trying to snap her back to reality.

"I… I don't know." She seemed to be having trouble focusing. "We were… were on a routine patrol through the low quarter, and as we passed by the gate we heard sounds. We followed them into the area and then we were attacked. We hadn't been here more than five minutes when you arrived."

"Fortuitous timing on my part, then," D'Arden said.

He took a step towards the soldier, and she instinctively took a step back. Her eyes were wide and glazed, and they darted down to the ground to fixate on the body of her fallen comrade, who had been split open like a ripe fruit by the demon's blade. There was blood everywhere, lying on the ground and mixing with the coarse black fluid from the bodies of the *zagoths*.

"I've... I've never seen so much bl..." she trailed off, and D'Arden thought that she looked distinctly as though she were turning somewhat green. His suspicions were immediately confirmed as she collapsed to the ground and began retching.

He took a step backwards.

Taking a moment to realign himself, he looked around the area. There were no signs of any other demons in the immediate vicinity, and for that he could be thankful. That would give him time to get the young soldier back through the gate to the low quarter and on her way to giving her report on the situation they'd encountered. If there were demons living here in the Old City, Captain Mor would want to increase the soldiers positioned in the area before things got too dangerous for the people. If he had the men to spare.

"Have there been many problems with demons in the area?" he asked her as she finally seemed as though she might be recovering, having expelled most everything that she'd eaten that day onto the ground.

"You're talking like... like this is just something that happens all the time," she said softly, still staring at the body of her fallen comrade. "But that's probably... probably true for you, isn't it? Oh, poor Jadzen..."

"I have seen a lot of death in my time, yes," D'Arden said, somewhat flustered and confused as to what that had to do with anything. "Death is, however unfortunate, a part of life. Your fellow soldiers died bravely fighting against an enemy that they had little hope of conquering even given proper time to prepare and plan."

"We weren't even supposed to be fighting," she said,

her voice weak and distant. "It was just supposed to be a routine patrol. Walk through the area, make sure the citizens aren't at each others' throats. There wasn't supposed to be any danger out here."

D'Arden frowned. He'd never seen a soldier so despondent at the loss of their comrades. It was painful, certainly, but this girl seemed to be in complete shock. He wondered if sending her off on her own to report back to the Captain was the wisest idea, especially if there were still *zagoths* in the area.

"How long have you been a soldier?" he asked, trying to bring her back to reality.

"A year, but we've never had to really fight," she said. "We've had to… to put down a few of the touched, and we've had to keep peace among the citizens, but there aren't any demons in Calessa! They're not supposed to be here!"

He didn't voice the idea that there was, in fact, a demon in Calessa, and it had been there for several years. The girl was obviously spooked already, and he decided that it would be wise not to make it any worse. Regarding these *zagoths*, though, she could be right. If they had not seen any demons before now, it would not make sense for them to be suddenly appearing now, unless the corruption was strengthening their resolve, making them braver.

"What do we do with their bodies?" she asked suddenly, looking up at him. Her eyes shone in the light of the Deadmoon, and tears were coursing down her cheeks. "We can't just leave them here!"

"I'm afraid we have little choice," D'Arden said as gently as he could. "There's no way that we can carry them anywhere from here. We can do our best to arrange them, but they'll have to stay here in the Old City."

"It's not fair!" she cried, slamming her gloved fists down onto the armored chest of the fallen man. "We were supposed to be going to get drinks together as soon as our patrol was done. We were going out to have a good time tonight… and now I'm the only one left."

Unstable was simply not enough to describe her. These young soldiers were not battle-trained nor experienced enough to know how to deal properly with death. This was likely her first brush with death, or if not, certainly her first encounter with sudden and violent death. He remembered having felt like that himself, once…

"Come," he said to her softly, extending his hand. "It's not safe out here for you alone. I'm looking to find why it was that I was drawn here, and while I believe it may have been in part to save your life, I don't believe that these demons are done, and that there are more lurking about. We should find them and destroy them so that they don't harm anyone else. Are you a fair hand with your sword?"

"Not top of my class, but I'm not bad," she said quietly.

"Good," he said with a nod. "You should accompany me so that you might achieve vengeance for your fallen comrades. When it comes to people, vengeance may not always be the best option, but when dealing with demons…" he paused for a moment, watching her expression. "It is always the best option."

As he watched, a fire seemed to alight in her gaze. Her eyes locked on his and she nodded. "Vengeance." She climbed to her feet and drew the sword from the scabbard that hung at her belt. "Tell me what I have to do."

"We can't go rushing headlong into battle," he cautioned, holding up one hand. "You'll need to follow me and do exactly as I say. This place is dangerous and there could be *zagoths* lurking around any corner. If you rush in too quickly, all you'll find is your own death waiting for you."

She nodded. "I'll do whatever you say."

Good. This one had a reason to follow him, to listen. He hoped that it would turn out better than his last association with a young Calessan soldier. There was still a dull ache at the thought of having lost Mikel to something so trivial, so minor… but such was life, and the thought drove him onward.

If the Old City needed to be cleansed of simple, mundane *zagoths*, then he would do so – and he would utilize this girl's sword to help him. He was fighting to save the population of this city, and it was obvious that they needed someone now who could fight an everyday problem as much as they needed someone who could fight the corruption that was spreading across their lands.

"Then we will find them, we will strike swiftly, and we shall destroy them," D'Arden said, nodding at the girl. "What is your name?"

"Elisa," replied the young soldier.

**

"Die!" she screamed as she dropped from several feet above the ground, a flying leap off of a crumbling stone wall. The steel of her blade flashed in the light of the Deadmoon as she descended onto the head of one of the unsuspecting *zagoths*, plunging the sword deep into the creature's body mass. It stiffened and fell forward, hauling her to the ground with it. It was clearly dead.

111

D'Arden took that moment to come out from behind a stone wall of his own, wielding his manna blade as though it were as light as a feather. The demons that were camped in the square had no idea what had hit them, and began scrambling for weapons even as D'Arden cut down two of them before they had a chance to move. A spray of thick black fluid now coated both of them, but neither of them seemed to notice.

Elisa dragged her sword from the body of the demon with a thick squelching sound and swung to face the next one. Out of the corner of his eye, he couldn't help but be impressed with the prowess of the young swordswoman. The thirst for vengeance that had alighted in her eyes drove each swing, and though they were amateur at best and she would have been soundly defeated in any kind of civilized battle, the place in which they were fighting was perhaps the furthest thing from civilized. The element of surprise lent them every advantage, and she cut down another even as he slew two more with swift and practiced cuts from the crystalline edge of the manna blade.

Within moments, all of the demons in the camp were dead, and for a moment, the only sound was that of the crackling fire they had set up to try and keep warm in the deep-rooted chill of the Calessan night. Elisa wiped some of the black sludge from her face and turned to look at him with a slight, feral smile.

"They don't last long when we get the jump on them, do they?" she asked, clearing her blond hair – now coated with *zagoth* blood – from her face with one hand as she leaned on her sword with the other. "Really, they're kind of stupid. It's almost like hunting animals, if animals had thumbs and weapons."

She was a bruiser, there was no doubt about it, and although her technique was raw and mostly unbalanced, he could see the potential for a half decent sword-wielder in her. If the situation were different, he might have been inclined to sponsor her to the Royal Fencing Society – a mostly outdated group now, but still the best place to learn the art of the sword, second of course to the Arbiter's Tower.

In fact, he said to himself, *if she makes it through this alive, I might just do that.*

He made the decision to see if, despite the hell that she was going through right now and the misery of their situation, she could be taught. He stepped up beside her and fell into a neutral sword stance, the blue crystal blade extending out in front of him at a slight angle from his body.

"Here. Mimic this," he said to her.

She fell in step with him, holding her blade in roughly the same manner. Yes, he could see it now. Her balance wasn't perfect, but she held the heavy steel blade with a natural talent and a good solid stance, and she appeared to be comfortable holding it. "From that stance, you can strike in any direction," he said, making slow movements with the sword in different ways, showing her all of the possibilities that existed with the one simple stance. "Try not to let yourself get off-balance. If you're not balanced, simply connecting with the enemy's blade could throw you off enough for them to get in a killing strike, and your armor won't help you if that strike hits your head or your neck."

She nodded, moving her sword in the same motions that he made with his, trying to get a feel for the more refined movements. "I don't want to die out here."

Her straightforward confession surprised him somewhat. Despite the bloodlust in her, she was still a frightened girl who'd been drafted into the town guard. She said it with such a calm voice, though, that it unnerved him further. "I don't intend to let you die," he said at last. "I'll make a bargain with you, in fact." *Might as well tell her your plan,* he thought. *Maybe it will help her get through this.* "If you live through this night, without any wounds that would seriously cripple your ability to wield a sword, I will personally sponsor you to the Royal Fencing Society in Hartsknell. You can leave this place, and go somewhere that you can learn to fight effectively and be taught well, and then if you still want to be a soldier, you can join up with the Royal Army and know how to fight properly."

"I'd go in a heartbeat," she said, a bit of the haunted look leaving her eyes. For the first time in their brief acquaintance, he noticed real excitement in her gaze. "I don't have any family left here… they've all died, or been turned and… and put down. I'd love just to get out of Calessa, and I've never been to Hartsknell. But surely a sponsorship to the Royal Fencing Society must be incredibly expensive!"

He nodded, but looked unfazed. "Expensive, yes. For one of your natural talent, though, a worthwhile investment. I have no lack of money, and I have little use for that which I have. To give you a chance to become a Royal soldier, or perhaps something else of your choosing, would be a worthwhile endeavor to me."

"We've just met, though!" she protested. "How could you think of spending that kind of money on a stranger?"

He shrugged. "I like your stance, and I find your bravery admirable. There is little more good I could do in this world than to get a talented young woman such as yourself out of this terrible place." He gestured at the crumbling stones around them, but really he meant to indicate the whole city. She seemed to get his meaning, and nodded.

She thought for a moment, and then locked her green eyes on his azure ones. "All right," she said. "I'll get through this. I'm going to hold you to that promise of yours."

"Good," he said with a slight smile. "I'm glad to hear that."

She lifted her blade. "Show me that stance again."

**

D'Arden had forgotten what it was like to have a student, a pupil, someone who looked up to him and hung on his every word. It had been years since he'd trained his last apprentice Arbiter, choosing instead to take every mission that would lead him across the land, hunting evil wherever it would take root. As this young girl stood beside him, though, mimicking his movements and showing real improvement even inside of a few hours, that memory began to rekindle. As he began to see more of Elisa's potential as a sword-slinger, he almost wished that she were younger, that he might be able to indoctrinate her as an Arbiter, rather than sending her off to become a soldier. The pain that he suffered, though, he would not wish upon anyone. The burden of the heartblade, the drive to fell evil at every corner and to seek it out whenever possible was

115

more than most could bear, and besides all of that, she was far too old to begin Arbiter's training now. If she were only a few years younger… but alas, this girl was not to be his next apprentice.

So instead he showed her every simple movement, every basic training in the way of the blade that he could remember. Obviously she was still too inexperienced for the more complex maneuvers, and some were downright impossible without the assistance of the manna, but many of the basics were the same no matter what kind of blade one wielded, whether it was steel, silver or crystal. Balance, leverage, proper swing arcs and stance were all things that he could impart on this suddenly willing student, and she absorbed all of it with alacrity.

They spent almost an hour in the dying light of the *zagoths'* fire, as the Deadmoon wandered through the sky overhead amongst the thin clouds that occasionally obscured its deathly white light. By the time they were finished, she was coated with a fine sheen of sweat and had shed most of her armor despite the cold. He had to admit, she was quite attractive even in the cold light, if several decades too young for his interest.

"The night grows long," he said. "We should take advantage of the cover of night to surprise more of these demons, if still they lurk here. You may not find all of the stances I've taught you to be comfortable, and more of them you'll forget before the night is out, but the basics should help you to strike stronger and faster at our enemies."

"I'll use them," she said with a nod. "Let's go."

**

Under the cover of night, they struck at several more camps of the *zagoths*. It seemed to D'Arden that Elisa's prowess with the sword grew steadily with each encounter, and with surprise on their side, they never suffered any wounds more serious than a scratch or shallow cut.

As the night grew to its darkest and the Deadmoon began to set over the western sky, D'Arden knew that it would soon be dawn. There was little to be gained by striking in the bright light, and the demons were nocturnal creatures, living their lives at night and crawling back into their holes by day.

They stood on the edge of the Old City near the dry riverbed, on the stones that had once made up the harbor district. The view of the eastern sky was clear, and he knew that the sun would be rising soon. The river itself was several yards to the bottom, but no water had flowed this way in centuries. It was hard to see in the dark, but he knew the land that stretched out before him which had once carried life-giving water to this place was now dry, cracked and parched.

"We won't find them once dawn comes," he told her as they picked over the remains of another slain camp of *zagoths*. "They'll vanish again in the daylight. They don't suffer from the corruption itself – these demons are entirely nature's creation – but they don't like the light any more than something touched by corrupted manna. The Old City will be safe for the day, and you should go and get some rest. It's been a very long night."

I should return to my manna font, he thought to himself. *I've expended enough energy this night as it is. There doesn't appear to be any real danger here in the Old City...*

the demons aren't brave enough to venture out of their territory now that we've decimated their numbers.

She nodded. There was a cut on her cheek that had already clotted, and there was a smear of drying blood. He hoped that it wouldn't scar and damage her lovely visage, but then again, he supposed, there were worse things than a real battle scar on a woman. "All right," she said. "I'll go back to the barracks. I could use some sleep anyway." There were thick dark circles around her eyes, and though some of the haunted-ness had left her eyes, he could still see the trauma of the loss of her friends lurking there behind her green-eyed gaze.

"Good," he said with a slight smile. "You made it through, just as I said."

"I told you that I would," she smirked. "You'll make good on that promise of yours, right?"

"I will," he promised again.

The first light of dawn began to break over the eastern horizon. Just as it did, D'Arden heard a commotion coming from behind him. He turned to look, and saw something horrific come out of the ground at them.

It was a massive spider, several times larger than a man, burrowing out of the ground. Dust and small rocks flew in all directions, and D'Arden could see the red glow surrounding it and the tiny red pinpoints in its multiple eyes indicating that it was a creature born and made of the corrupted manna. He wondered how many of these spiders there might be even as he backed up, holding one arm out to keep Elisa behind him.

"It's a manna spinner," D'Arden said breathlessly as it came fully into view. The huge black carapace was unmistakable – this was no ordinary spider, but a creature born to swim the underground currents of the manna, normally benevolent and non-aggressive, now twisted in its corruption as it came out of the ground near them. He wondered briefly why it might be emerging just as the light of dawn was breaking, but he had little time to wonder.

"Die, beast!" Elisa was shouting as she raised her sword high in the air and rushed at the creature.

"Elisa, no! You can't…"

Too late.

As she swung the sword hard, it bounced off of the manna spinner's hard body and reverberated so hard that the steel blade almost cracked. She was stunned by the sudden rebound of the sword and staggered backwards. D'Arden leapt forward to help her, but even his assisted speed could not help him as the manna spinner sank its giant, manna-tainted fangs deep into her body. She cried out and stiffened as the manna-venom coursed through her body, and collapsed like a marionette as its strings were cut as the spider withdrew its deadly bite.

"Damn you!" he cried, leaping forward and drawing the crystalline sword from his back in the same motion, bringing it slicing downward through the air. It caught one of the spider's outstretched legs and severed it on contact. The blue manna fire devoured the severed extremity within seconds, but the beast was able to resist its effect as the azure flames attempted to creep up its extremity.

It hissed at him – a deep, terrifying sound – and struck back, stabbing at him with clawed legs. He swung at them as they came by, but the spider was too swift when it was paying attention to him, and he wasn't able to connect with either one as they passed by. He danced forward and struck again, but the spider pulled back, moving just out of his range and lashed out at him once more, trying to push him off guard so that it might have a chance to bite at him as well.

He could hear Elisa, lying on the ground a few feet away and moaning softly. Each successive breath was getting weaker, and he could hear her heartbeat slowly draining away. Each beat took successively longer, and with the help of his manna-tuned hearing, he could hear every labored beat as the corruption began to take her over. He didn't have long to deal with the spider if he had any hope of saving her.

What hope is there? He asked himself in despair. *She's been touched by manna, and corrupted manna at that. What hope is there for life after such a wound?*

His mind provided him with the answer. *The heartblade.*

Could he do such a thing? Could he supply her with a tiny dose of purified manna, a boost against the corruption that now flowed in her veins, without completely killing her? Would the dose be too large and begin the manna transformation, or would it be too little to save her from the horrid fate that had befallen her?

Fighting with the idea in his head, he struck again at the spider, this time connecting solidly with its carapace. Where the steel blade had bounced, his blade sank in, and the spider let out a hideous shriek as ichor spouted forth, luminescent, like the kind that had come from the fel dog he'd fought outside Calessa's gates. He yanked the sword free and spun away as the spider attempted to sink its fangs into his shoulder, narrowly avoiding a poisoning himself.

As the beast dripped its luminescent fluid on the ground, D'Arden could tell that it was beginning to slow.

It fought with less certainty, less precision as it lashed out at him, and D'Arden knew that he'd struck a deadly point on the beast. Its attacks began to seem less and less like coordinated strikes and more like death throes.

He moved in for the kill. As he stepped closer to the spider, one of its flailing strikes caught him squarely in the chest.

D'Arden gasped. The world seemed to slow to a halt.

Slowly, he looked down. The beast's clawed limb had hit him straight on and had punctured straight through his chest, his ribs, breaking bones and tearing through muscle and soft organs as it went. Blood and manna flowed out from him as he tried to catch a breath, but found that he was already feeling faint from a sudden lack of oxygen.

The spider yanked back its appendage and staggered backward, finally falling over the edge into the dry riverbed as it twitched frantically, trying to slow the loss of its vital fluid. It vanished into the darkness.

He fell to the ground slowly, in a motion that seemed very well to take an eternity. He hit the ground with such force that it would have driven the breath out of him, had he not already lost the ability to breathe.

D'Arden clawed at his belt, hoping that he had saved some sort of potion, some sort of alchemical substance that could save his life. His fingers closed only on the hilt of the heartblade.

The Arbiter weakly unlocked it from its specialized scabbard, and brought it up to his eyes. The thrumming of the light in the heartblade was weak. It would not be enough to inoculate Elisa against the poison running through her and also to give him the strength he needed to force the manna to repair the wound he had sustained.

There was no other choice.

He would have to let Elisa die.

With a desperate cry, he thrust the blade deep into his own chest, little caring if he sustained more damage. He was dead anyway if this didn't work, and he had neither the time nor the strength to make a careful application.

The thin, round blade pierced his heart.

Time stood still for a long moment.

The manna in the heartblade flashed into his body. Immediately the manna took hold of his body, wrapping around him in a warming embrace and beginning to knit the flesh that had been horribly wounded by the spider's attack. He only hoped that it would work quickly enough before his mind died of air starvation.

Black sparks began to flash in front of his eyes and he felt himself slipping away, the pull of the manna on his soul getting stronger with every second that ticked by. His heart beat weaker, and weaker. He struggled to draw a breath even as he felt the uncomfortable itch and burn of the flesh repairing itself thanks to the burst of manna. Fear gripped him; fear that it wouldn't be enough, that it was already too late for him, that his failure would cost the world dearly.

His lungs inflated.

Desperately, he gasped for air, reveling in the taste of the sweet dawn. The pull of death faded from him, and he found the sudden strength to pull the heartblade free of his chest.

As he held it up in the light of the rising sun, it suddenly illuminated with a brilliant flash of azure manna energy. He stared at it as it pulsed in his hand to the rhythm of a heartbeat not his own, uncomprehending. He had just expended what little energy it had held contained within it, and yet here it was, glowing as though it had just been recharged.

A low, weak moan snapped him out of his daze. He scrambled to his feet, doing his best to ignore the sharp flashes of pain that he felt as new flesh that had not completely healed tore and blood flowed again. He rushed to the side of the fallen girl and knelt beside her.

Elisa's skin already had a dusky grey tint to it, and her face was ashen. Her green eyes were a strange, almost surreal splash of color against her otherwise colorless form. They stared at him, not quite vacantly, but with so little recognition that he feared it was already too late. The blood had stopped flowing from the deep wound in her shoulder, but it mattered little. The venom had obviously spread like wildfire, and even though he had no idea how long he'd been semi-conscious, Elisa was nearing death.

He held up the glowing heartblade in front of her eyes. Her glassy gaze focused on it with a vaguely puzzled look. "This is the only thing that stands a chance of saving your life," he told her, though he knew that she likely could not understand him. "The chance is very slim. I have never heard of such a thing working before. It is probable that you will die."

She nodded, weakly, once.

"Do you want that chance?" he asked her.

Again, weakly, she nodded.

Needing little more of an answer than that, he unbuckled her breastplate and pulled down her shirt, just enough so that he could get access to the area above her heart and not enough to expose her to the chilled morning air. He took the pulsing heartblade and slid it carefully between her ribs.

She gasped, and the blade thrummed in his hand as it released its charge of power into her. He removed the heartblade quickly from her, leaving a trail of blood and tiny blue flames behind.

Her entire body buckled as she screamed, the sound echoing throughout the broken-down buildings that surrounded them. He gave a soft thanks to the land for the daylight that would keep the demons from pursuing them, even though it would now be clear to their entire population exactly where they were. The pure manna was coursing through her bloodstream, obliterating the corruption that had been forced into her by the spider's bite.

Now was the moment of truth. If she survived the initial purification, she might still stand a chance. He waited, more nervously than he would have expected for a life he'd come in contact with so recently.

As her scream finally died away, her body went completely limp. Her eyes stared blankly out across the dry riverbed.

He bowed his head.

After a few long moments, he reached out and grasped her wrist. There was no pulse, no indication of life. He'd lost her to the purification.

D'Arden breathed a heavy sigh. He'd known the risks when he offered it to her, and even if she hadn't understood them fully, she had some idea of what it might have done. It could have been much worse, he thought – she suffered none of the transformational effects that normally accompanied a direct exposure to manna energy. The regret that she hadn't survived, though, weighed heavily on him.

He'd hoped that no matter how slim the chances were, that this young girl might have survived where the young boy Mikel had fallen, that he might have had the chance to make amends for the boy's senseless death.

The sun continued to rise over the horizon.

**

He carried her body through the labyrinthine rubble that made up Old Calessa. She was light in his arms, less weight than he would have imagined, even without her soldier's armor. He would not leave her corpse there to be ravaged by the demons, though he left most of her possessions behind. She was dressed now only in a thin white shift, as he'd left behind most of the padded under-armor as well, deeming it unnecessary for a simple burial.

At last he passed under the gate that led him back into the low quarter, having kept careful tabs on his direction this time so that it would be possible for him to find his way back again. He had little desire to carry her all the way out to the recently purified graveyard outside of town, as it was nearly a mile back to the trade gate and then another hour's walk from there. He decided that he would simply offer her to the purified manna font in the low quarter, and allow her body to be dissolved and returned to the land, just as had happened to Mikel.

He walked the streets of the low quarter in the early morning's light with a grim face and a solemn demeanor. D'Arden had little love for death, though he encountered it on a frighteningly regular basis. His least favorite death of all was that of the innocent, of the talented, and of those with the greatest potential, for it felt as though it was those who were truly wasted. It was one thing for the farmer who'd toiled all of his long life to finally return to the stream of life, but it was quite another for a violent and unexpected end to come to a young life.

At last, he approached the door of the font chapel.

Something was wrong.

He felt it spreading outward from behind the door, a sickening, twisted feeling that struck him to the core. Someone, or something, had undone all of his work. The corruption radiating from behind the door was even stronger than before. He'd lost his foothold, he'd lost the boy, and now he'd lost a swordswoman with incredible potential that he'd expected would grow into something great.

Everything was lost.

What was he to do? He could not comprehend who or what could have corrupted this purified font so quickly, in just one night. Something horrible must have come past here and attempted to induce corruption into the font purposefully, otherwise it would have resisted simply something passing by.

He had an enemy here, and one that was smarter and more dangerous than he'd imagined. The guard captain, Mor, had mentioned that there had been an Arbiter here who'd succumbed to the corruption several years previous. D'Arden doubted that even the demon himself couldn't have poisoned a font so quickly. The corruption that was carried by true demons was insidious and deadly, but it was slow to work and only the most powerful of demons could wield it so directly.

The mysterious Arbiter, whoever he had been, was a far more likely culprit for this sudden corruption. What had Mor said? *"When he was finished clearing out the old fort, he descended into the catacombs beneath it, and never came out."*

He needed to discover if there was anything left of the Arbiter who had visited Calessa those years ago. A corrupted Arbiter was dangerous, but if there was indeed one who had turned so fully and given so completely into the siren song of the corruption, and had wallowed in it for so very long, the danger would be astronomically high. He almost envied the girl who lay peacefully in his arms, for she would never have to see what horrors might lie below that old, abandoned fort.

The girl needed a burial, or at least for her body to be dissolved by manna energy, so that her energy could return to the land from whence it came. He had expended much of his during the night, and what little had remained in the heartblade had purified the corruption from her. He had not enough within him to purify her body completely so that it might rejoin the manna stream.

D'Arden felt as though he may as well simply throw himself into the corrupted manna font and die, dissolved and destroyed by that which he fought. He had no desire to carry the girl's body through the trade quarter during the day, where it would be seen by all, and he had no way to give her the proper respect here, which he truly felt as though she deserved.

He set down Elisa's body on the cobblestones – gently, of course – and clicked the heartblade free of its specialized scabbard at his belt. He drew it forth and examined it, looking for any sign that it had regained some of its power. The light deep within the rounded crystal thrummed faintly, but there was so little that it would not even guide him into his trance state, much less fully dissolve a human body.

The Arbiter strained his mind, searching through it for some historical footnote that might give him some indication. His heart still yearned to save Elisa from the fate that had befallen her, and so he hoped that he might find something in his memory that might still help her. Unfortunately, he found no such idea anywhere in his mind, to his deep regret.

There was nothing to be done for it, he decided at last. He would have to take her body to the graveyard outside of town, and utilize the manna font there to send her properly on her way.

Resolute at last, he picked her body back up into his arms and began to walk.

**

He was forced to stare straight ahead as he passed back through the trade quarter, carrying the limp and ashen form of the young girl who'd died only a few hours before. It was still the early morning, and D'Arden hadn't slept the entire night previous. His arms ached from carrying her the last mile through the streets of Calessa, and now the stares of the townsfolk burned into him as though flames shot from their eyes.

He was carrying the body of one of their own – that much was obvious by the shock of blond hair that tumbled from her head. Her green eyes were closed, but he knew that behind those soft eyelids and dark lashes, those eyes stared blankly outward, dead to the world.

D'Arden passed through the gate without a word

to the guards who stood there, those who obviously recognized Elisa as one of their own and stood in silent mourning and acknowledgement. They were soldiers, not citizens – they realized that the price of freedom was vigilance, and that vigilance sometimes required sacrifice. They bowed their heads as he passed, and the gate was opened for him as silently as possible. It closed again behind him as he cleared it.

The Arbiter began the long trek to the graveyard where he'd encountered the risen corpses of Calessa's dead. It was there that stood a manna font, one mostly untouched by the corruption now that he had purified the area, and where he might offer the girl's body properly to the land that it might return to the flow as normal, and not become twisted or reanimated again by the evil that permeated the city.

By the time he reached the cemetery at last, his eyes burned in the morning sun, and the muscles in his arms were on fire. Each step was a staggering lurch as his strength began to give way, all of his special augmentation having been burned away in the combat of the previous night. He was now little more than a man, a man with a task, a man with a mission. Sweat dripped from his forehead in rivulets only to freeze moments later in the frigid air. Each forward movement was a blinding agony, and once the graveyard finally came into view over a small rise, he gave a soft cry of relief and joy. The journey was nearly done, and he would need some time to rest before he would be strong enough to hunt down those responsible for the corruption in Calessa, for he now had a clear idea of where the next part of his investigation would take him. His desperate mind had cursed him soundly for undertaking this extra leg of the journey out of respect for a dead girl that he had met only hours before, and cursed him for wasting time when the corruption still spread, but a deeper, more instinctual part of his mind drove him onward, driven by the hunger, the need for something right and true to happen in this awful place.

When finally he reached the manna font that stood in the graveyard, complete with the wall of force that he'd erected to keep unwitting passerby from passing through the deadly light of the energy, he collapsed to the ground with a cry. The girl's body struck with force that he'd not intended, but he no longer had the strength to keep himself upright, much less her dead weight as well. He weakly lifted one hand towards the font and dropped the energy he'd been silently expending to keep the protecting wall in place, and it vanished.

Refreshing, warm azure light spilled forth from the entrance almost joyfully, suddenly released from its prison. It fell across both of them, and instantly D'Arden felt his strength begin to return to him. His aching body was soothed by the warm, regenerative light of the font, and the exhaustion that ran through the very core of his being began to abate as the manna fed him, replenished him and once more lent strength to its servant. He breathed in deeply, taking in as much of the energy as he could muster in a single breath, feeling the warming relief flood through his veins and his body. Sanity began to slowly return to him, and his gasps for air slowly became instead sighs of relief.

Once his breathing had returned to normal, D'Arden dared to force his body into a sitting position. There was pain, to be sure, and it was sharp, but it was nothing like he'd imagined it could be. Already the exhaustion was fleeing him as he was buoyed once again by the power of the land that he'd been trained to accept in place of his own energy. His body no longer would regenerate on his own; wounds would not heal and fatigue would not leave, not since the balance of power in his body had tipped from his soul to the manna itself. The miles-long walk had been terrifying to him, knowing that if he had not reached the font in time, he would have been powerless to stop his own death.

Strength returned to him more rapidly as he was able to control his breathing, taking in the energy from the manna and centering himself, beginning to replenish his stores so that he might once again have the strength to fight evil. He would need to trance for several hours to make sure he was properly strengthened to go back in and face whatever waited for him beneath the old Calessan fort, but he no longer felt that it was an impossible task.

He lurched to his feet once again, after only a few minutes had passed. Once more he took up Elisa's body and approached the font. With the greatest of care, he laid her form across the crystalline structure of the land's energy vent, all the while feeling more and more of his strength return to him. Once he was satisfied with how she was situated there and ensured that her body would not fall to the ground, he turned away and stepped outside the font, letting the radiance warm his back and allowing the manna to take its time returning the girl's body to the land.

A piercing shriek from behind him caused him to spin around rapidly. His eyes fell upon her just in time to see her leap up from the font and back away towards him, breathing desperately and in a full-blown panic.

He was stunned; how could a pure font have raised this child's body from the dead and reanimated it. His hand immediately went to his sword, ready to strike the creature down where it stood, no matter how much it might pain him to do so.

She turned around rapidly, and just as D'Arden was about to draw the sword and cleave her head from her shoulders, he got a full look into her frightened green eyes. No pinpoint of corruption lay there, no hint that she was nothing but a reanimated corpse. Full emotion – fear – was present on her face and she looked at him as a wild, cornered animal looks at its aggressor, her blond locks plastered against her face and her skin pale, but no longer the white of death.

Elisa screamed again before collapsing on the ground before him, unconscious but clearly breathing.

D'Arden could do nothing but stare.

V
CONFRONTATION

The Arbiter's mind spun uncontrollably. How could something like this have happened? Elisa had been dead for hours, he had felt her body stiffen as the soul had fled after the heartblade had failed to save her…

The heartblade. Could its power have had something to do with this?

The artifact that was the very continuation of an Arbiter's existence, that piece of utmost importance had been created centuries ago by the greatest sorcerers of the time. It was the key to the creation of an Arbiter, and it was the key to their survival. They could bathe in manna to replenish their strength, but in order to continue living and continue their resistance to the power of the manna's energy, the heart itself needed to be regularly exposed to the power of the energy, something that was impossible from the outside. The tapered pinpoint blade was the only way to do that without risking severe injury to the flesh and stopping the heart cold.

Despite this knowledge, however, the true power of the heartblade remained something of a mystery. The design specifications, the method of creation were all known by the Arbiters and they could be created at the Arbiter's Tower, but exactly what the depths of the concentrated power could achieve was beyond comprehension. The heartblade was not to be used on any except a fully ordained Arbiter, and yet he had broken that rule, and achieved… what?

Could this now have brought the girl back from the

dead?

Still the light from the manna font fell upon her unconscious form, and yet still she lay there, unmoving but breathing steadily, unchanged by the power of the radiant energy that should have been twisting her form to suit what lay within, and robbing her of any life that remained in it.

He knelt down beside her and placed a hand on her shoulder. Her eyes fluttered open, and slowly she turned herself to look at him. The fear had mostly gone from her now, but still she looked uncertain, a small amount of the previous panic still remaining in her gaze.

"I was… I was trapped in there!" she said, her voice barely above a whisper. "I could hear, I could feel, but I couldn't see once you… once you closed my eyes! I heard everything that the townsfolk said to you, but it was like I was frozen, and I couldn't move or tell them that I was okay…"

His brow creased in a slight frown. "How do you feel now?"

"Warm…" was all she answered.

D'Arden looked to the blue light from the font that radiated down upon them, and he felt the same. He felt the warmth that the land offered to its servant, the light that infused him and made him feel both loved and as though he belonged perfectly, as though nothing could ever be wrong or separate him from that power.

Had he unintentionally created an Arbiter?

"Elisa," he said softly, brushing the hair from her eyes. "I need you to do something for me. Can you stand?"

She slowly nodded, and began to push herself to her feet. A few seconds later she stood facing away from the font, looking only slightly unstable, and quickly adjusted her awkward stance so that she was standing more comfortably upon the uneven ground. She looked down at herself, noting that a majority of her clothes and her armor was gone, and immediately flushed with shame and embarrassment.

"Elisa," he said again. She looked at him, and there was still a bit of the wild uncertainty in her gaze. "I need you to turn around."

"I'm afraid to," she whispered.

"Turn around," he urged.

He could see her tense, unwilling to move for a moment, and then she turned, the blue light of the manna font illuminating her face fully. She stood there, and D'Arden waited expectantly, still with the thought that this could all end in a moment, and she would be gone again as quickly as she'd returned.

Nothing happened.

"It's so… warm," she said, staring into the light.

He stepped up and placed a hand around her shoulders, guiding her forward. She gave some resistance at first, but then she relaxed and allowed herself to be pushed closer to the almost blindingly-bright light. With one hand he grasped her right wrist, and as they approached the font he reached out her arm to touch the crystalline structure. He wrapped her fingers around it, and she gasped.

A piece of the crystal broke off in her hand as though it was little more than dirt. It came free, a long, slender piece drawn from the ground to exactly the proper length, and though it cut her hand and blood flowed and she cried out, the blood that dripped forth burned with tiny flecks of blue flame.

He had created an Arbiter.

This event invalidated many of the things that he'd been told about the creation of an Arbiter from the masters. He'd always been told that the exposure had to begin at a young age so that the human form could become accustomed to the energy, and that it took a period of several years before they could Draw their first manna blade from the earth. Here it was, it had been merely hours since her first heart exposure and she had already Drawn.

It was incredible, it was beyond comprehension, but the truth stood before him in a radiant white shift, glowing with all of the power of the manna. There were things about his profession that had been lost to history, and this was apparently one of the more dangerous – and also potentially useful – that had been found once again.

And for all of that, he thought bitterly, *the Elders will almost certainly have us both executed for blasphemy and heresy.*

He pulled his manna blade free from its confines with its rasping sound, and gently guided her to face him. Still her blood ran in rivulets down the crystalline shard that she held in her right hand, and it burned and infused the crystal with her essence just as it had done for him all those years ago. He grasped his own blade with his free hand, slicing deep into the flesh, and then placed it over hers so that their blood ran together down her new sword. There was a bond between the student and the master that ordained them that, according to teachings, could not be invalidated by any means.

But now, he was forced to think, *Can I really trust any of those teachings?*

"You are ordained an Arbiter," D'Arden whispered, his

voice still incredulous. He repeated the words of the creed with little intervention of his own mind. "Search out evil and corruption. Strike it down with the power of purity. Keep your mind and your body free of corruption, walk the path of the righteous, and forever strong you shall be in the light of the manna."

She stared at him with her green eyes that now also glowed blue with the light of the manna. The words that had been stated by every ordained Arbiter since the beginning of their order, the words urged by the manna and by the flow of the land tumbled almost unwittingly from her lips. "In the light of the manna I serve."

D'Arden couldn't help it – he smiled. In the face of everything, the corruption that permeated this city and the danger that still lurked within it, he smiled. He had found a light here, a light that would go on and would not be extinguished. A new Arbiter, accidentally discovered and added to their order by the virtue of simply trying to save the life of a talented sword-slinger. Now there was another voice, another sword of light to battle the darkness that was ahead. She was untrained, she was still rough with the sword and she was young, but she would learn, and the power that they shared would stand against any darkness that might impede their path.

The smile faded. He could not share with her the lurking dread he felt about their return to the Arbiter's Tower; it would have to remain silent and hidden for now. Perhaps his fears would not come to pass.

With concentrated effort, D'Arden shook off the gloom that threatened to overwhelm him, and forced the smile back to his lips.

"Come, Elisa. We have much to do here." He held out

his free hand.

She grasped it with hers.

**

Their return to Calessa was nothing short of triumphant. Where hours before there had been curses muttered in low tones and looks of anger and rage and betrayal, now there was reverence, something that could be almost described as worship. One of their own had died in the line of service and had returned to them, a feat which was beyond the impossible. The light from her manna shard radiated outward onto the faces of those who clamored to see the dead returned to life in radiance, instead of onto expressions of mixed awe and fear.

He had guided her through her first trance, and she'd shown remarkable ability. Once they returned to Calessa, he retrieved an extra blade wrapping from his saddlebags, and they'd clothed her at a tailor's shop in a manner which was appropriate for a fledgling Arbiter – flowing, unrestricting clothes of white and grey. The white symbolized the purity of the newly pledged, and the grey showed the long road ahead. He also gave her his spare sheath, and within an hour upon their return to the city, she looked all the part of an Initiate.

Once they were done, D'Arden looked over his new protégé with an eye for detail. "It's not the right cloth, but it will do. At least the look is appropriate. We will have to fetch you proper clothing once we return to the Arbiter's Tower. I'm afraid you won't be going to Hartsknell after all."

"I'd rather stay with you," she said softly.

"And so you will," he replied. "There will be time for formal training in the future. Right now, there is an evil that threatens Calessa and all of its citizens, and though you are no longer one of them, you bear the same responsibility to them as you always did. We must find the evil that is corrupting this city and raising the toll of dead with every passing day."

"Where do we look?" she asked him.

"Right now, we look beneath the old Calessan fort, in the north part of the city. There was an Arbiter who visited this city five years ago, according to your guard captain, and he told me that the Arbiter disappeared beneath that fort into the catacombs beneath. Though we strive for purity in all things, some of our number do fall victim to the corruption. Those who do need to be destroyed at all costs, for one who falls to the corruption wielding such power as we do are a dangerous foe indeed," D'Arden told her.

"Do we stand a chance against an enemy like that?" she asked.

He nodded. "We are two, and he is one. Though you are new to your power, still our combined energy will be stronger than his corruption. We will find him, and we will purify this place so that life may return to normal before we leave here."

She fingered the wrapped handle of her new manna blade gingerly. "The blade is so light – will I know how to use it?"

"You will find it more comfortable than the heavy steel you swung about previously. It is lighter, it is faster, and it is several times more deadly, especially to those who fight from the side of corruption. We must be careful, though, exposing you to such danger so young. If I had a choice, I would leave you to await my return, but I cannot. I will need your strength as surely as I will need my own."

Elisa nodded, though it was somewhat tentative.

"Come, child," D'Arden said with a slight smile, a warm expression that he had not used in several years – the approving glance of a teacher to a student. She responded to it immediately, by looking shyly away with a broad smile. "We go to the old Calessan fort to discover the source of this evil."

**

They approached the broken ruin that had once been a proudly standing fort many years previous. D'Arden remembered from that time that there was talk about sending an Arbiter to Calessa to destroy an evil that had inhabited this old place, but he had been on mission at the time, and was not informed about who had finally been sent.

It would have had to be someone powerful, he thought as he gazed upward at the ruined spires. The place was impressive and awe-inspiring even in its broken and run-down condition. The manna currents curled around and flowed through it, turning red and raw as they touched the building and passed along its side. He heard Elisa draw in a breath beside him.

"I've lived in the shadow of this place my whole life, but I've never seen it this way before," she said softly.

"The currents tell us many things that the normal eye cannot see," D'Arden said, following her gaze as it traveled up the dark towers that reached toward the cold blue sky. It was incongruous, the vision before them, of a silhouette which was not a silhouette, black stone against the clear and cloudless blue that caused a sharp contrast, with the blue and reddened manna flowing within and without, ebbing and flowing all around them in its desire to permeate and find the shortest path for complete immersion. "This place has much corruption within its walls. It will be dangerous within; there may be many demons, many dangers lurking inside. I realize that your skills are lacking, Elisa, and this will be both frightening and harrowing for you. The corruption may tease and tempt your conscience and your soul, daring you to step out of my protective circle so that you might embrace a long-lost loved one, but you simply must ignore these visions. They are as unreal as a dream, and a thousand times more dangerous."

"Will it try to tempt you as well?" she asked him innocently.

D'Arden clenched his jaw firmly for a long moment, his eyes looking through the fortress as though at something far in the distance, and then answered, "Yes."

Without another word, they proceeded forward up the black stone stairway that led to the desiccated door which would take them inside. His instincts screamed at him to leave this place, to run and hide. Crossing this threshold would be like crossing into the land of the dead itself, and he did not relish that thought.

For a few moments, they simply stared at the open doorway, leading inward into what looked like a very normal stone reception room or cloakroom. D'Arden held out one hand cautiously, and lifted the other to draw his manna blade from the sheath on his back, which came free with a low rasp. Only a few seconds later, there was another, slightly higher rasp as Elisa drew her own manna blade free from her back. The pure energy that radiated outward from their blades helped to keep back some of the corrupted manna that flowed around them, making him feel ill. She was still young enough that the feeling of the corrupted manna would feel like power to her, instead of noxious.

He would need to keep a close eye on his new protégé.

"Come, Elisa. There is nothing to be gained by standing here on the landing," D'Arden said, as much for his own benefit as for hers.

Together, they stepped through the doorway.

Immediately a feeling of claustrophobia set in on them. It was dark, and the light from the cold sun outside had vanished entirely as if it had never existed. It felt as though the walls were pressing in on them, though he could feel nothing. The light from their blades was reduced merely to a dim glow, barely visible even for their brightness in normal conditions. It reminded D'Arden uncomfortably of the darkness in the cellar of the low quarter, but far more constricting.

He felt Elisa beside him struggling to breathe. He laid a comforting hand on her shoulder as he tried to regulate his own air intake, and she seemed to breathe a little easier when she felt his hand on her.

They took a step forward, and then another. D'Arden tried to remember what the room had looked like from outside, but the utter inky darkness erased all memory of the place from his mind. It was only when he found his outstretched hand pressed up against a cool stone wall that he could even remember that he had a hand.

The darkness seemed to be pressing in further, weighing on his mind in such a way that might make him forget who he was, if he stayed within it long enough. The corruption in this place was unthinkably bad, and if he'd been able to read any of the fonts in the city at all, if the whole city hadn't just blended into one horrid puddle of twisted manna, he would have known to come here first. That thought made him dread even worse, for if there was indeed an Arbiter down here who'd embraced such terrible power, this battle was going to be more difficult than everything he'd been through over the past few days combined.

Finally, his groping hand found the doorway, and he pulled Elisa through it along with him. When they reached the other side of the threshold, the pressing darkness vanished, leaving them standing, panting desperately for air, in a circle of radiant blue light. He looked over at Elisa, who returned his gaze with a nod.

He believed that she might be beginning to understand what was in store for them.

D'Arden looked around this next room, wondering what could possibly lie ahead of that deep, despairing darkness, and how much they would have to endure to reach the self-appointed master of this dismal fortress. He dared not voice these thoughts aloud to Elisa, for her own fear was great enough without knowing exactly what sort of horrors might lie ahead for them.

"Elisa," he murmured softly, his voice echoing unnaturally in the room. "Be on your guard. We don't know what might be next." She deserved at least that much of a warning. He saw her nod with acknowledgement.

Without warning, the room suddenly filled with

a chattering sound that was so loud, it drowned out all hope of communicating verbally with each other. They stood back-to-back like two surrounded wolves, each guarding the flank of the other and holding out their blades protectively as the volume of the sound reached near-unbearable levels. It at first sounded intelligible, then began to blend into a sound like a thousand voices speaking in ancient, forgotten tongues all at once, and then became a sort of strange insectoid buzzing that filled their ears. Elisa might have cried out, but D'Arden could hear nothing over the horrendous noise.

Then, from out of the darkness, they came. Demons of all shapes and sizes, at least a dozen of them, as this sound echoed all around them in the room. The demons approached slowly, with lopsided, slavering grins on their faces. These were minions, not deadly, but certainly dangerous to his acolyte. The cacophony was not just distracting, it would cause one to make a fatal mistake if they were not careful.

He shouted an order to Elisa, but it was lost amongst the sound of tens of thousands of buzzing insect wings in their ears. Making sure to stay where he could feel her presence or see the glow from her blade, he struck outward at one of the slowly approaching demons, who easily rolled aside, out of the way of his attempted attack. They closed in ever closer in a deadly ring. Though it would be dangerous for her, he could not help but silently thank the land for providing him with a second blade that could fight against the corruption. It would make all the difference, he knew, in this encounter and every encounter going forward into this awful place.

That was, of course, assuming that she didn't get

killed.

It became more difficult even to hear himself think as the sound seemed, impossibly enough, to grow louder. The sound was supplemented by the thick smell of rotting flesh and decaying bone, most likely whatever it was that these demons had eaten last. One of them approached too closely, and D'Arden struck outward, catching the demon squarely in the shoulder with a passing cut. The demon shrieked – at least, he imagined that it did – as the blade cut through the flesh of the arm and ignited a purifying fire there. These were no mundane demons, these were creatures spawned wholly from the corrupted manna that permeated this place, and they had little to no resistance against the azure flames from his manna blade. They took root in the wound immediately, consuming outward in a rapid blaze that flared up brightly as they dug into the demon's body, wriggling into every gap in its armor in an attempt to purify all of the evil within.

It staggered backwards, its mouth hanging open, exposing a deep black throat and ragged yellow teeth. The cobalt fire leapt down the demon's throat as it left that entryway open and exposed, devouring the beast from the inside out. It collapsed to the ground as the manna fire ate at it from within, its face still frozen in what appeared to D'Arden to be a silent mask of agony.

One down, still a dozen to go.

His head was beginning to ring from the impossibly loud buzzing sound that surrounded them. He forced his brain to stay focused on the task, trying to focus on the sound of blood in his ears to drown out some of the outside sounds, but to little avail. His only choice, then, was to strike quickly in hopes that he could destroy the demons before the buzzing disrupted his thinking too much.

Immediately he struck outward again, and another of the demons – which had apparently in no way anticipated an attack at that moment – was caught by the edge of his manna blade. It was just deep enough to leave a long red slit across its throat below its disgusting visage, and the manna flames ignited in the same second, burrowing inward, seeking the corruption that lay within. The demon stumbled away from him, screaming in the same silent agony that he imagined would have been much louder, if he could have heard it at all.

His attacks became a dance of sorts, a series of flowing movements with the most deadly intent. He struck and they parried, and he moved to strike again or to strike another. Each of his movements flowed perfectly into the next, and though the buzzing in his ears was almost deafening him, he began to imagine that he heard a rhythm in the sound that he used to time his movements. *Cut, step, strike…* the pattern of movements took him back to his fencing days at the Arbiter's Tower in the clean warm air, in those golden days of youth that are always remembered fondly. He struck down demon after demon, the blue flames igniting eagerly at each successful stroke, consuming the demons from head to toe in a matter of seconds.

As suddenly as it had started, the noise ceased.

His head continued to ring. The sudden silence was almost more deafening than the noise itself. He turned to find Elisa, down on one knee and holding her sword almost desperately before her, shaking her head to try and clear it of the ringing that remained behind.

"Are you all right?" he asked, and his voice sounded strange as it echoed in the stone chamber.

She nodded slowly, and then climbed back to her feet. Bright red blood showed on her tunic from where a demon had cut her across the arm, but she showed no other obvious injury. Acolytes always wore white, so that injuries could be more easily spotted. The manna would not start to heal her wounds automatically for several years yet – in the meantime, she would have to rely on her body's natural healing ability.

"What was that awful sound?" she asked.

He gave a half-shrug and shook his head. "I have no idea. That's the nature of this place, though… it will do whatever it can, whatever it has to, so that it can win the fight. Whoever – or whatever – is the master of this place does not control these happenings any more than you or I can. These are creations of the corrupted manna, spun from whole cloth in order to drive out the purity that's crossed its gates."

"What might be next?" she asked, a hint of fear in her voice.

"I don't know," was all he could answer.

The doorway that led back to the room of perfect darkness was visible, and there was another doorway directly across from them that led into yet another unknowable chamber. Anything could lie beyond that threshold – even the certainty of their own deaths – and yet he was compelled to travel onward, to discover what had brought this place so deeply into corruption, and to drive it out.

He glanced at his young student, who returned his gaze bravely. "Are you ready?"

"Will I ever be ready to take that step?" she asked rhetorically.

"I'll let you know if I ever get there," he said grimly.

Together, they stepped across the next threshold.

Flames surrounded them. D'Arden could feel their heat, blinding him and searing his flesh. He heard Elisa cry out beside him. The fire had not been there only seconds ago, but now it was all too real. He could feel his skin as it blackened and burst where the flames touched him. He gave a shout of agony as well that echoed in the chamber above the sound of the roaring flames.

He got a glimpse, ahead of them, of a doorway that seemed impossibly far away. The floor was made of hot coals and embers, and fire flared all around them on every side. The heat was so intense that he felt as though he might simply die on the spot. Sweat poured from every part of his body and yet it was immediately evaporated. There was no way to survive.

This was the end.

D'Arden clenched his hand down on the sharp edges of his manna blade. Blood surged forth from the wound, and he cried out yet again. The pain from the wound in his hand, however, made the flames in the room flicker slightly. He felt cooler, and the azure fire of the manna blade danced around him. His flesh no longer felt as though it were being seared. He could still see the flames, but they seemed more distant somehow.

"Elisa!" he cried out. "Let pain be your guide!"

He heard her sob to his right, and he turned to look. She had collapsed to the ground, and though he could now see that she was suffering no real injury, she truly believed that she was. The illusion here was very strong. She had given up screaming now, and was only barely whimpering.

She was not strong enough for this.

He knelt down beside her as the flames continued to retreat for him, their heat dissipating rapidly. D'Arden took hold of her hand and sliced his blade along it, drawing a thin line of red forth. She yelped, a pitiful sound of the dying caused yet more pain, but he could see that the heat was beginning to fade for her as well.

Slowly, she sat up at last. There was a haunted look in her eyes that reminded him of the night they had first met, which seemed far longer ago than it was. "Is this the kind of thing you deal with every day?"

"Not exactly," he admitted. "I haven't encountered this much corruption in many years."

"When was the last time?" she asked.

"Mount Tzoggoth," he replied immediately, offering a hand to help her up.

She accepted it and rose to her feet, a bit unsteady but otherwise looking unharmed. She gripped the handle of her manna blade as though it were her only lifeline, and perhaps in a way it was. She was still not fully attuned to the blade, and it would take a few years of training before she would completely understand its power, but for now her simple prowess with the sword would be enough.

They approached the next doorway. As D'Arden looked through it, he saw only what seemed to be an endless procession of doorways attached to square stone rooms. They appeared to go infinitely into each other, vanishing eventually into the darkness. He shook his head. He did not know how long that they would last with these trials. Eventually, an illusion would fool himself or his student completely, and they would be lost forever inside the bowels of this ancient fortress.

Laughter echoed through the stone halls, its source unseen but the sound unmistakable. It was not maniacal laughter, not the laugh of the truly mad, but instead the cold, calculated sound of a mastermind who was enjoying the results of his plan too well.

"Are you enjoying my maze, little ones?" a voice asked.

The Arbiter's head snapped around as he searched for the source of the voice. It sounded all too familiar, and the words sunk deep into him and filled him with a dread that was entirely unspeakable, a feeling that could not be put into words. His knees felt weak, and sweat began to bead on his forehead.

Elisa looked at him strangely. "Are you all right?"

D'Arden felt as though it was difficult to breathe, and there was no illusion causing that feeling. He coughed, and the light from his manna blade flickered angrily in response to his sudden stress.

"We're in a lot of trouble," he murmured when once again he could finally speak.

"Do you know that voice?" she asked.

"Yes, tell her, D'Arden," the voice mocked from its ethereal position. "Tell her that you know exactly who was sent to Calessa five years ago. Tell her that you know exactly who I am, and what I intend to do to the both of you before the day is out. Tell her all the things she wants to know, because in a very short amount of time, she won't be hearing anything any longer."

"Who is it?" Elisa asked, a note of fear rising in her voice.

"I haven't heard that voice in many years," D'Arden said softly, his brain still stammering uselessly as the realization of exactly what he was in for sunk in. "It's been almost twenty long years since I've heard that cadence, those words, that voice. There was a time when it would comfort me, when it would reassure my fears away, and when I might have felt better for hearing it.

"Now my heart fills only with dread, and with sorrow, for many questions have now been answered, but so many more have become apparent."

D'Arden took a step forward and held his head high, bringing up his manna blade before him and staring deeply into the light, hoping there to find some sort of comfort.

"Come out, Havox Khaine!" he intoned, making his voice as deep and confident as he possibly could. "Drop this ridiculous charade and make some semblance of the honor that you once carried as a member of our illustrious Order! Stop hiding behind your traps and your illusions, you coward! Come out and fight!"

"Are you sure that's what you want to do?" Elisa asked as the disembodied laughter echoed around them once again. "Who is he? Who is Havox Khaine?"

D'Arden bowed his head.

"My mentor. My teacher. My... friend."

The stone room dissolved around them, and suddenly D'Arden saw through the illusion as it began to fade. The tiny stone rooms had never existed at all; in fact, they had fallen right into the trap laid by Khaine, the man who'd been his first Master as an Arbiter – the man who'd taught him nearly everything he knew about wielding the manna blade, purity and the danger of corruption.

They stood instead in a great chamber, with crumbled remains lying where before the stone walls of the interior of the fortress had stood. They had obviously been demolished in an effort to create what was in fact some kind of massive, twisted throne room.

Before them stretched a long staircase, constructed entirely of glossy black stone that resembled obsidian, but glowed softly with an ominous red light. It sparkled in the light in tones of red and orange. His eyes traveled up the massive stairway to the top, where sat his mentor, the first person who'd ever spoken to him in an official capacity as an Arbiter, the man who'd trained him and put him on the course to righteousness and purity, in a giant throne made of red and gold. So massive was the throne itself, so arrogant was its presentation that Khaine himself nearly disappeared when the entirety of it was viewed as a whole.

"Do you like my kingdom, young one?" Khaine's voice boomed in the chamber, echoing and reverberating several times off of the walls. "Soon all of Calessa will be under my control, and then my power will spread farther yet. No more will the Arbiters bow a knee in fealty to the broken throne at Hartsknell. We shall rule with an iron fist, and the manna shall transform all who resist into our servants – or else they shall die. I have discovered true purity, my student – true purity lies in absolute power."

"So that wolf I slew in the low quarter truly was your servant," D'Arden sneered, finding no trace of the man he once respected and loved as a father in the apparition that sat before him. "It too spoke of power as purity. You are lost, Khaine. I may once have been your student, but this student has become more than his master obviously could ever have become. I have surpassed you. My dedication is to the land, and your 'purity of power' is killing this land and its inhabitants. What is power if there is no one left alive to rule over?"

Khaine laughed, a terrible sound that at once reminded D'Arden of the kindly laughter of his mentor and the screeching sound made by a demon all too amused by its prey. "Power is in the hand of those who hold it, Tal. You would not dare to stand against the power that I wield now. It is only with power that we can truly be free. You ask me what is power? I say that it is the ultimate goal of life, that which can only be attained through the death of those who stand in your way. Tell me, Tal, do you stand in my way?"

"I do," D'Arden said, his voice proudly defiant.

Khaine clucked his tongue reproachfully. "I thought that you had much potential, D'Arden, when you were my student. I see now that I taught you the lessons of the Arbiters all too well. You cling to their false ideals like a child clings to its mother's teat. You were not fit to be my apprentice."

The figure rose from its seat atop the dais and slowly began to descend the staircase. As it came into view more closely, D'Arden could see that it was in fact the image of the man he'd loved so dearly. The same red hair, though it was graying around the temples. The same kind eyes, though they had been hardened and carried many more wrinkles now than they had the last time D'Arden had seen the man. Once an apprenticeship ended, an Arbiter was not likely to see their mentor again unless there were some kind of extenuating circumstances.

D'Arden wished they'd met again under different ones.

"What about your little acolyte there, Tal?" Khaine asked him. "Does she see the world the same way you do? How long has she been an Arbiter? Does she know that the

Arbiter's Tower has sent her to her certain death?"

"I've never been to the Arbiter's Tower," Elisa said before D'Arden could stop her. D'Arden mentally smacked his own forehead. There was no way that Elisa had been properly prepared for an encounter of this magnitude.

Khaine's head tilted in an approximation of surprise. "You hold a manna blade. You wear the robes of an acolyte. Tell me, child, how is it that you have never before been to the Arbiter's Tower?"

Elisa looked toward D'Arden for some sort of help, having realized that she'd said something wrong. He gave her a shrug in return; there was no helping it now. The truth might as well come out.

"I've been an Arbiter for less than a day," she said, somewhat bitterly. D'Arden ached for her, having to face a confrontation like this so soon after her ordainment. Acolytes needed training; he'd been a fool to bring her here.

Khaine's eyes blazed with interest and amusement. "How is that possible?"

"I have no idea, Khaine," D'Arden said, echoing the bitter tone of Elisa's statement. "She'd been bitten by a manna spinner. I gave her a dose from the heartblade to try and save her life. When I offered her body to the font, it revived her instead of dissolving her."

"Interesting," Khaine mused, stroking his chin. As he approached closer, D'Arden could see that the cool blue eyes that had once belonged to his mentor were gone entirely – instead there blazed bright red light that usurped the entirety of his eyes. He was built more powerfully than D'Arden remembered, his arms bulging with muscles and blazing with strange red tattoos that appeared to be some sort of ancient language, all alive and burning with the power of the corrupted manna that had overtaken him.

"What say you, little one? Do you still stand beside him now that you have seen the power that I wield?" Khaine finally reached the bottom of the staircase and reached out one hand towards Elisa. She stiffened, but wisely she did not move as the disproportionately large hand stroked her cheek almost tenderly. "You have none of the training that my misguided former apprentice carries, none of the values of 'purity' and 'light' that would keep him from attaining all of his goals in life in a matter of moments. What say you?"

D'Arden felt himself tensing with rage also, his knuckles turning white as they gripped the handle of his manna blade. How dare he touch her with his corrupted fingertips, allowing the corrupted manna to flow through her? D'Arden knew though that Khaine well understood what he was doing; Elisa was not properly exposed to the pure manna yet – she'd only had two doses from the heartblade and would barely be considered an infant by the standards of the Arbiters. She was much more susceptible to his corrupted touch.

"Get away from her!" D'Arden shouted, swinging his blade at Khaine. The older man stepped backward quickly, and the blade sliced through the air only inches from Elisa's face. She flinched backwards and stumbled a step or two away as the manna blade cut through the air before her.

Khaine laughed again at his ineffectual attack. "You see, dear child," he said to Elisa, "This is what those values achieve and attain: nothing more than a blind attack that could have just as easily taken off your head as mine."

D'Arden found rage welling up inside him. This man

had been everything to him once, and now he was openly mocking the very ideals he'd taught D'Arden to believe in. He struggled to fight back the anger, knowing that it would only blind him to Khaine's next illusion, whatever it might be.

"I knew they'd send an Arbiter," Khaine said, studying one hand dispassionately. "Of course they would, once they felt my power growing here. I never expected, though, that they would send you, Tal. Did the Grand Master even tell you that I was the one who'd been sent here five years ago? Did they even begin to hint at what you might find here in Calessa?"

"Of course they told me," D'Arden lied boldly. "I knew exactly what was going on here, and so did they. In fact, I volunteered to come here just so that I could be the one to put you down."

Khaine laughed again, and the sound boomed off the walls. "Such a brave boy, lying to your Master like that. The manna tells me more than you would ever imagine, Tal. Did you know that once you learn to see the manna clearly, you can see how it changes in a person? Even the poorest, most miserable of peasants has manna within them, and that manna can be changed or it can be manipulated, and those people can be utilized in ways that you would never imagine."

"That's ridiculous," D'Arden spat. "Only the Arbiters have enough manna within them to be read. The amount of manna in the normal person is miniscule, undetectable even by the most well-trained eye."

Khaine wagged a finger at D'Arden reproachfully. "Oh, how little you know. The manna itself is within everything, within everyone in the same amount. Arbiters have no more manna inside of them than anyone else."

"You're not making sense, Khaine," D'Arden said, narrowing his eyes. "Of course an Arbiter has more manna within them. That's why the heartblade exists, that's why regular exposure to the fonts is so necessary. That's how we survive, by tipping the balance of our bodies and our souls toward the manna."

Elisa was merely standing back, a few steps away, watching the two of them. There was fear in her eyes, and she seemed to be regarding both D'Arden and Khaine with the same amount of fear. That only enraged him more. He was supposed to help this girl, now that he'd inadvertently cursed her with the heartblade. This was supposed to be her chance for a better life. He'd be lucky if she would ever let him near her again after an experience like this.

"You're wrong, Tal." Khaine said this in such a way that brooked no argument; it was not a counter to D'Arden's statement, but simply a statement of fact. "The heartblade is a special enchantment. It does not contain manna, but instead an agent that at once both lends resistance to the deadly energy of raw manna and forms an instant addiction that cannot be broken. It draws you back to it with its own energy, requiring you to take sustenance from it. The manna from those fonts is killing you as surely as time is killing you. It dissolves your being, a tiny mote at a time, relieving you of your humanity until one day your soul is swept away in the font, and you are gone forever from this place.

"Don't you see, Tal? The manna is not pure or corrupted. All of it is deadly. Every exposed font in this gods-forsaken world is deadly. All of it is corruption, and we are all a part of that corruption. Humans are not meant to live in a world like this, we are not meant to exist in a place with this kind of energy. The Arbiters simply fight to keep the balance tipped towards the side that they have chosen, so that they can more easily control the power of the land to their own ends. Once my power spreads and all of your 'pure' manna is driven from it, new things will grow in the shadow of the Red.

"Men will adapt, just as they always have."

D'Arden fell back a step, thunderstruck. He could not believe the words that were flowing from the mouth of the visage of his old mentor, and yet somehow, everything seemed true. His head was reeling. If any of this were true, it would invalidate his entire existence. Everything he had fought for, bled for, nearly died for would be completely gone.

"What about Calessa Heights?" D'Arden demanded. "That is not adaptation! That's nothing but madness!"

"An unfortunate side effect of a cleansing fire is that some things get burned," Khaine replied patiently. "There were some there who did not respond to the power of the Red, and it spread like a sickness. The good Captain Mor was good enough to board up the place to keep it from spreading further – after, of course, he spoke with me."

Damn it! D'Arden cursed himself inwardly. *Even Mor is in the pocket of this monster! How did I not see it?*

A broad smile spread over Khaine's face, revealing wickedly sharpened teeth. "I see you realize the depths of your plight now, Tal. Yes, I have been watching you since the moment you stepped foot in my city. At first I was amazed that they had sent you, so naïve and so unwitting into this place. Then, as you began to realize just what was going on here, I began to get angry. I had Mor plant that boy with you, all the while intending that he would die, to see if I could break your resolve." The smile darkened into a dangerous frown. "I see now that it was pointless. Instead, somehow, you found one of the few who my power had not touched at all, and somehow cast her dice in your favor, though it is supposed to be impossible."

So even Khaine hadn't known about the heartblade's secret; that it could even change someone later in their life and give them the power of the Arbiter. That helped D'Arden to feel slightly better, and he was able to pull back his blinding rage from the edge of a foolhardy attack on his enemy. He stole a glance at Elisa, who was still watching the both of them fearfully, and shook his head.

"Words are words, Khaine," D'Arden said at last. "You stand here before me and speak of things of which you have no way of proving. It matters little how much your words ring of truth. Even if they were lies but you believed them fully it would change the manna in your favor, and the both of us know it."

"Would you then like a taste of my power, Tal?" Khaine grinned wickedly once more. "I would be happy to demonstrate it for you."

D'Arden lowered himself into a combat crouch, gripping the handle of his manna blade tightly in both fists. "Show me."

Khaine reached to his back and pulled free a sword that was unlike any manna weapon D'Arden had even seen. The blade was twice as wide as his own, and curved wickedly near the end, glowing brightly with the red light of the corruption. It shone on both himself and on Elisa, and he did his best not to flinch as he felt the twisted power rain down upon him. Instead he focused his own energy into his manna blade, brightening the glow of the pure blue power that he wielded in order to fend it off, and took a step closer to Elisa so that she might benefit from its protective shield as well.

"Not so fast," Khaine said with a smirk, throwing out one hand. A burst of crimson light shot forth from his fingertips, rocketing toward Elisa with incredible speed. She let out a shriek that was cut short as the light surrounded her.

D'Arden whirled around, but she appeared unharmed – simply immobilized in a glowing cage of red power. "What have you done, Khaine?"

"Simply removed an element from the equation," said the monster which had replaced the man he'd once known. "Her soul now hangs in the balance, Tal. Do you have the strength to save her?"

"My power is stronger than yours," D'Arden said evenly.

"I will show you my power!" Khaine bellowed. His strange blade shone brightly, almost white-hot at the center, and his eyes did the same. He drew back with both hands and struck forth at D'Arden wielding that strange and terrible blade. It was a slow and clumsy attack, and D'Arden knew that his opponent was capable of better. He brought up an almost disinterested parry to easily deflect the oncoming stroke.

When the blades met, D'Arden felt a shock run through his bones that he'd never felt before. The two sides of the manna were warring within him. He nearly cried out in agony as pain filled him like never before. He wondered if his opponent felt the same, but when he looked upon the face of his former mentor, twisted and changed by the corrupted manna, he saw there only malice and no signs of weakness in the unnaturally-stretched grin.

D'Arden shoved the other blade away from him, and as they disengaged, the feeling of the war inside him dimmed but did not vanish. He had no time to recover, though, as Khaine began to press the attack in earnest. No longer were the strokes slow and cumbersome – that had obviously been a ploy to show D'Arden the exact extent of the power that he was up against. Now they were rapid, blows flying in quick succession, and it was all D'Arden could do to get his blade up in time to defend each one. He tried to take the moment of defense to analyze his opponent, to find some sort of weakness in his defense, but the pain that lanced through him every time he parried a strike made it difficult to concentrate on anything but each successive attack and counter.

Khaine's attacks were each a deadly stroke, and there were some that D'Arden only parried just in time to save from his chest being pierced or his neck from being severed. He managed to get in a few counterattacks, but they were weak and Khaine easily batted them away. D'Arden quickly realized that no matter what his prowess with the blade was, Khaine's corrupted energy was assisting him in a way that the pure manna never could. D'Arden did everything he could to draw on his reserves, but the corruption that filled the very air around him prevented him from drawing any more from anywhere. Khaine had a limitless supply of his own power, and D'Arden had to carefully manage his own so as not to expend too much of it, lest he be left completely powerless before this madman.

With each step backward he took, a realization became more and more clear to him. He was losing this fight, and he stood no chance on this uneven ground where his opponent wielded so much more power than he.

"Khaine!" he shouted, his own voice echoing in the chamber, though not so much as his opponent's manna-assisted bellows did. "You coward! You would never be fighting me if you weren't in your own, self-appointed kingdom! You know that my power is stronger than yours, and that's why you fight here, on this uneven and biased ground! You're not fit to be any sort of king – you're nothing but a wretch who can't stand the thought of being beaten!"

"Fool!" Khaine roared, pressing his attack even harder. D'Arden felt his arms weakening – if he could not get his opponent to stop this assault he would be dead in seconds, not minutes. "You think that since you cannot best me with the sword, that you will best me with words! Ridiculous!"

"Come on, Khaine," D'Arden sneered, trying not to let the weakness in his voice show through. "It's not even a contest, here in your palace. You know you're going to win. Wouldn't you rather prove your power in a place where I actually stand a chance?"

Abruptly, the relentless assault simply stopped. Khaine took a step backward, lowering his blade and staring into D'Arden's manna-blue eyes. "Ridiculous as it sounds, Tal, you're right. It is pointless to fight you here. Perhaps if you see the truth of my power, I will not have to kill you. Perhaps once you see the truth, you'll join me instead of fighting me."

We'll see about that, D'Arden thought, but said nothing aloud.

"You propose an Ether battle, then?" Khaine asked.

D'Arden nodded. "There's no other way to truly prove it. On the ground we're either firmly in your territory or mine. If you really believe that your Red is stronger, then prove it in the only place where neither one of us has an advantage."

"You're going to die, Tal," Khaine said, once again sporting that terrifying grin. "Once you die, or decide that the proper place is with me, the Arbiters won't be able to stand against my power any longer."

"Then so be it," D'Arden shrugged, acting disimpassioned. "If that's the will of the land, then that is what is shall be."

"The land knows nothing but what it is told," Khaine said angrily.

"We shall see," D'Arden answered.

They stepped back from each other, and for a moment, simply regarded the other, as if expecting some sort of treachery. At last, they each sheathed their respective weapons. D'Arden glanced at Elisa, and she met his eyes with less fear now, and nodded, still holding her manna blade. It was clear that Khaine regarded her as no kind of a threat, and had simply ignored her so far in the battle.

Despite what Khaine had said previously, D'Arden did not believe that their power was simply two sides of the same coin. He had seen the death and the destruction that the corrupted manna had caused. The angry red glow did not speak simply of a different kind of purity. The madness that seemed to engulf all that the corruption touched – the living corpses, the rising dead, the insane fel creatures that walked the world – did not speak of purity of any kind, but only of evil and of danger. Though he was saddened by the loss of his mentor to this terrible power, he knew that he could not waver in his resolve simply because he now fought against someone that he had once known.

Havox Khaine was gone. In his place was a monster, nothing more than a fel beast.

D'Arden hoped that he could continue to believe that.

They lifted out their arms together. The Ether battle was an ancient tradition, a duel between Arbiters who could not settle their differences. Battling in the Ether meant that neither side had direct access to the power that drove them; they had to summon it, to draw it to themselves and wield it. Their physical bodies would be left behind; there would be no blades, no strength – only energy. It was the final rite of passage to be fully ordained as a Master Arbiter. D'Arden thought that he must be the first Arbiter in many centuries, and possibly in time, to fight the Ether battle against a corrupted Arbiter.

The world began to fade around him as his spirit rushed towards the Ether. He felt Khaine's presence following him, only a second behind. They would meet in the Ether, and D'Arden would wield the power of the pure manna against his foe. If he could not win here, then the world was truly lost.

They arrived in the Ether; a nebulous place that appeared as though they existed in a cloud. It was grey, ever-shifting and never the same for more than a moment. Looking into it was like looking into a thick fog; one could see a short distance and then everything simply faded to gray.

D'Arden saw himself in the Ether as an azure beacon of light and purity, and this is how he appeared. Every movement left a trail behind him, and he appeared like a shining star, blazing as brightly as the sun.

Khaine appeared in the Ether a moment later, and appeared to D'Arden as a bright red fireball, full of anger and hatred. He burned even brighter, blindingly white at the center and fading to orange and red flames toward the outside.

There were no words in the Ether, no taunts could be exchanged, no strategies revealed. There were only feelings and flashes of light exchanged between the two parties, and somehow there always seemed to be a kind of implicit understanding.

The battle was begun.

D'Arden summoned up the power from the land beneath him, drinking and drawing in the purity that he could feel from wherever he could feel it. It mattered little where the power came from, and he shaped it into a shield that he held before him. Only seconds later, Khaine's first attack slammed into the shield and exploded in white and red around him. He was driven backwards from the force of it, but the shield held firm.

He drew in another stream of power from the land below, and shaped it into a lance that he hurled with one hand at his opponent. It flew straight and true like an arrow sent sailing from the finest bow, but the red energy leapt up and devoured it before it ever reached its target.

To any spectator who could have witnessed the event, it would have appeared that two stars had decided simply to battle it out in the heavens. The Ether was invisible from the world and could not be viewed by normal means, but D'Arden was certain that the Arbiter's Tower was aware of the conflict. He made many of his attacks as spectacular as possible, hoping to draw the attention of his fellow arbiters so that even if he fell, that they would know of his valiant efforts to stop this corruption before it spread further, and so they might also be aware of the danger that faced them if he should fail.

As the battle raged on, D'Arden became aware of the fact that he was winning. Explosions rattled the Ether where the two of them fought, but it became clear to D'Arden that he was slowly winning victory over his opponent. Khaine's attacks began to lose power – not all at once, but each attack seemed to be progressively weaker, while D'Arden felt himself growing stronger each time he tapped the land for its energy. He could not fathom how exactly that he was winning, only that he was, and he rejoiced in the victory. If he could truly defeat Khaine's corrupted energy here in the Ether, he would be severely weakened back on the mortal plane, and D'Arden would be able to extinguish the corruption in Calessa once and for all.

He continued to throw attacks at Khaine, drawing more and more energy from the land to beat down his former mentor's corruption. He'd lost all hope of purifying the man, to bring him back from the insanity – if D'Arden had come here years ago, he might have had a chance to save Khaine from the depths of the corruption, but alas, he knew that it was now too late.

Suddenly, D'Arden could no longer feel Khaine's presence.

Had he won?

He rushed back down to the mortal world, relinquishing his hold on his spiritual form and racing back towards his body at alarming speeds. He crashed back into his body just in time to see a grinning Khaine driving the wickedly curved manna weapon towards his heart.

He hadn't won.

Khaine had resorted to treachery.

The world seemed to slow to a crawl. Khaine's death grin face bore down upon him, the glowing red blade coming closer with every second that ticked by. It was at critical mass – there was no way that D'Arden would be able to draw his sword and block the attack. In the face of his power, his former mentor – the most honorable man that he'd once known – had opted out of losing in the Ether battle and had come back here to drive the sword through D'Arden's unwitting heart.

There was no honor, no power in Khaine's desperate attack.

It pained D'Arden deeply to be defeated by it.

He could not be defeated by it.

Drawing on every ounce of strength he possessed, D'Arden twisted aside and the blade merely sliced along the flesh of his collar and the base of his neck, drawing blood and cobalt flames from the wound. It was no fatal blow like Khaine had intended, but the pain that flared in his chest disrupted his concentration. He stumbled away, rolling along the ground before regaining his feet, somewhat unsteadily.

They circled each other for a moment, and then D'Arden stepped in with his manna blade and cut downward at Khaine. It looked like a simple downward cut, and Khaine gave a horrible grin as he moved to parry. Instead, D'Arden changed his sword's trajectory at the last moment, slicing under his opponent's guard. Khaine tried to block, but could not bring his sword to intercept in time. The blade sank deep into the flesh of Khaine's shoulder and alit with the azure flames. The larger man stumbled backward with a shriek of agony that rumbled the very foundations of the building as blood flowed and the blue fire consumed the droplets.

He pressed his attack then, aware of his growing advantage. Short one arm, which now hung limply by his side, Khaine's parries were slower and his attacks less effective. D'Arden was as clearly winning the sword battle as he had been winning the Ether battle.

A perfectly-timed swing by D'Arden disarmed his opponent. The red manna blade skittered across the floor to rest several feet away, and D'Arden planted one heavy boot in his opponent's chest, sending him to land backward on the marble floor. Blood was flowing now both from the deep wound in his shoulder and from multiple other shallow wounds that D'Arden had inflicted.

He stepped up then to stand over his former mentor, whose eyes still blazed with the red flames of the corrupted manna. "I'm sure you're very proud of yourself, Tal. That was quite the tricky attack with your sword. Where did you learn something like that?"

"I'm not proud at all," D'Arden said, staring into the eyes of his former master, ignoring the jibe at his swordsmanship. "I am disgusted, humiliated and disappointed that the man who once trained me and taught me everything that I know has fallen to such a low level." He placed one boot firmly on Khaine's chest as he began to struggle and pressed downward until he felt the sternum begin to snap. "I am revolted by you. This is your elegy, Khaine. If the Arbiter's Tower wasn't already aware of what you'd become, thanks to the Ether battle, I would come back to them singing your praises about how you had waged a war against the corruption and fallen bravely to it, fallen in battle like a true warrior. I alone would have carried the burden of your madness, your corruption – the burden of all of those who have died under your watch. Your arrogance has driven you to this, your hubris was your downfall. I am not proud. I do this only because I must."

"Then you will rot in Hell itself!" Khaine said, grabbing hold of D'Arden's boot and shoving him backwards. Khaine scrambled back and once again took up his blade, fighting with renewed vigor. He was drawing again on the power of his palace, and D'Arden could see the wound in his opponent's shoulder healing. Soon Khaine was fighting with two arms, and D'Arden found himself in the losing position once more. He cursed himself for talking instead of taking the chance he had to end this madness.

This time, it was D'Arden who found himself disarmed. His manna blade clattered to the ground, and though it was not far from him, there was no way that he could retrieve it without Khaine impaling him.

"As it should be at last," Khaine said, lowering his blade only slightly. "The master has outperformed the student. I win, Tal. It's over now. You and your little bitch die today, and I will personally cut the hearts out of every one of the Arbiter's at the tower. Your power will feed mine, and when I finally control an army of undead Arbiters, the world will fall at my feet!"

D'Arden felt despair rising in him. How could he have failed, when he had come so close to victory? It seemed hopeless.

He could feel the corrupted mana flowing over him,

seeking a way past his defenses. It had been hours since his last spark from the heartblade, and he feared that the corruption might find a crack in his mental armor.

Could he beat Khaine, he wondered, if he let the corruption in? Was it possible to use Khaine's own power against him?

For the briefest of moments, he considered the possibility.

Then it was too late.

Khaine's curved manna blade drove through his chest. Explosive agony filled his world. He tried to scream, but it only came forth as a ragged cough. Blood and traces azure flame danced on his lips.

He could feel the life draining out of him as Khaine's power surged through him, consuming the blue fire that drove his life-essence.

His mind became suddenly clear. If he was going to die here, he did not intend to let Khaine win.

With one hand, D'Arden grasped Khaine's blade, close to where it had entered his chest. He forced his other hand to wrap around the blade farther up.

"What are you doing?" The corrupted Khaine stared at him, red eyes wide.

Using every ounce of strength he could muster, D'Arden dragged himself along Khaine's blade. He felt the crystal scrape against his ribs, and more blood and azure flame poured from the wound.

"When did this happen to you, Khaine?" D'Arden gasped. "What changed you from the man who taught me?"

Khaine was so shocked that he hadn't moved. He simply stood there, dumbfounded, staring at D'Arden.

Once again, D'Arden dragged his body along the blade. Closer.

"What evil touched your heart so deeply that you chose the path of corruption?" D'Arden's voice was ragged, labored. He stared into the eyes of the man he'd known and cherished, searching for some sign that he might still be in there.

There was nothing. Only madness.

"I have done nothing but open my eyes to the truth of the universe," Khaine sneered, though D'Arden could see a flicker of panic in the elder man's insane glare.

"I don't believe you. *What happened to you, Havox?*"

"Just die!" Khaine shrieked.

Khaine wrenched his sword around and released the handle, dumping D'Arden and the blade onto the ground. D'Arden wrapped his hands around the hilt and tried to wrench it from where it had lodged in his breastbone, but the conflict between the red energy that flowed from Khaine's crystalline sword and the pure blue manna which filled D'Arden's veins was too strong. His fingers were weak, slipping along the edges as he tried in vain to pull it free.

"My power will consume you in short order, Tal," Khaine said, turning away. D'Arden looked up weakly, watching as crimson flames crept over Khaine's body, healing his wounds and restoring his strength. The blade lodged in D'Arden's chest burned with the corrupted power as it sought to overcome his will. The pure manna which pulsed within him refused to succumb, battling against its opposite. He gasped desperately, trying to pull air into his damaged lungs, but he could not breathe.

Khaine turned to the immobilized Elisa, and with a

gesture, released her from her prison. D'Arden watched helplessly as she collapsed to the ground on her knees, breathing heavily. She struggled to rise, but he could see that Khaine's power was beginning to overwhelm her.

"Now you see the truth, little one," Khaine said, raising his arms expansively. "Now you see whose power is the stronger."

Elisa looked up at the twisted monster before her with wide eyes, glowing with the azure fire that D'Arden had instilled in her. "I see."

Agony gripped D'Arden's mind, agony stronger than that which immobilized his body. He closed his eyes for a moment, and then opened them again to watch.

Khaine approached Elisa, dropping his bulging arms back to his sides. "There is a greater power here than you imagine. You, who have only been introduced to the manna within the last few days, have a greater potential than any who have been suppressed by the heartblade. It is more than a drug, you know… more than anything, it is designed to limit the power of those who are gifted with the ability to see the manna flow."

D'Arden strained to see Khaine, to see if perhaps his former mentor was telling lies, but Khaine's back was to him. The heartblade was designed to *limit* his power? How much could he have gained without it?

"So… I could be even more powerful than you?" Elisa asked.

"Indeed," Khaine said, nodding his grotesque visage sagely. "You may become my apprentice, child – follow me and my power, and we shall remake the world in the image we desire. My power is limited – but yours is without constraint. All it requires is time and training."

Elisa rose to her feet slowly, still gripping her crystal sword in her hand. The cobalt power within her radiated outward as an aura, but as D'Arden watched, it began to slowly take on an amethyst cast. She was succumbing to temptation.

Khaine laughed – a horrible sound which echoed off of the walls of the chamber, ringing in D'Arden's ears. It felt as though his brain might begin to bleed as the monstrous laughter infected his mind. "You see, Tal? Even your apprentice can see the truth! If only you could have seen it before I was forced to kill you!"

D'Arden felt his vision beginning to darken. With Elisa losing her focus and willpower, the last bastion of his own power was rapidly disappearing. He was going to have nothing left to draw on shortly, and then he *would* die, vanishing forever into the flow of corrupted manna which had taken over the city of Calessa. Khaine would be victorious, and all would be lost.

Khaine turned back to D'Arden, staring down at him from his massive, inflamed height. "You should have accepted my offer, Tal."

"Never," D'Arden managed to spit.

"Fool!" Khaine thundered. "Even now you refuse to admit that my power is the greater?"

"Forever, Khaine. You are... a failure," the Arbiter wheezed.

His former mentor's red eyes blazed hot white. "A failure, am I? Who lies dying upon the floor, and who stands victorious? Who failed to stop me from conquering Calessa? Who is the one who refuses to see truth when it stands before his very eyes?"

"You failed... your ideals. You failed... your friends.

You failed… me," D'Arden choked out around the pain in his chest.

"I have seen truth!" Khaine proclaimed righteously. "I have seen the truth of the universe, and now you will die without ever seeing it for yourself!"

"You may be right, Khaine," D'Arden said, though he felt himself disappearing rapidly. He was going to die. "But there's something you… didn't count on."

"What?" Khaine demanded.

"You overplayed…your hand. Overestimated… your power."

Khaine laughed again. "I've done no such thing. I've won, Tal. What could I have possibly overlooked? I've…"

He never saw the blade that Elisa drove down through the back of his neck, severing his spine and protruding from a point just above his navel. Khaine stopped mid-sentence and gave a choking cough. He looked down to see the blazing blue crystal of Elisa's sword sticking out amid blood and crimson flame.

Azure fire rolled off Elisa in waves. Any trace of violet was gone from her blazing aura, replaced by the pure blue of the uncorrupted manna font.

Khaine dropped to his knees as Elisa drove her sword further through his body. He choked again, blood spouting from his lips as he opened them.

"It was me," she said, her voice cold as midwinter.

D'Arden met her eyes over Khaine's shoulder, and he gave her a weak, but approving nod.

Cobalt fire burned over Khaine's entire body, rapidly consuming the crimson that tried to fight back. As Khaine toppled over to the ground, Elisa rushed past him and knelt down beside D'Arden.

"I'm going to… die," he gasped.

She stood once more and, with both hands, grabbed the protruding handle of Khaine's curved manna blade, and placed one foot against D'Arden's chest. She pulled with all of her strength, and though D'Arden gave a hoarse cry of agony as she did, the sword scraped free of his breastbone and came away covered in blood and weak curls of blue fire.

Elisa tossed the blade away, where it landed several feet from both them and Khaine.

"Don't die, D'Arden," she said, kneeling down beside him again. "You can't die. I just saved you."

He coughed. He was able to draw on her power once more, but it was too late. He could feel himself beginning to slip away. There was not enough power within him to heal the deadly wound. It was a miracle he had survived this long.

"I'm sorry, Elisa," he whispered. "The Tower is to the north. Go there, and…"

"I'm not going anywhere without you," she said fiercely. With one hand, she reached into his vest and fished about, finally pulling free the heartblade. It glimmered weakly, the corruption having leached the power from it as he lay there.

"There's… not enough," he said.

"Like hell there isn't!" she exclaimed. The heartblade glimmered brighter. "There damn well better be enough here to save you, because I am *not leaving without you.*"

D'Arden watched as the glow of the heartblade slowly changed from the tiny glint of a faded star to a blazing white light nearly worthy of the sun itself. "Elisa…"

How was she doing that? The heartblade could only

be recharged on a font...

There was so much he did not understand.

She concentrated on the tiny, needle-like dagger until the light from it was enough to hurt his eyes. Then, without a word, she thrust it into his chest.

The spark from the heartblade leapt into him as though he'd been struck by lightning. His body spasmed and pain flooded him again, but this time it was not the pain of death. It was the pain of life.

Familiar, warming blue flame began to creep through the wounds he'd suffered as the heartblade's power began to knit him back together. It was excruciating, but he could slowly feel life returning. His breathing began to ease until it no longer pained him to draw in air.

"It worked," he said, and the words didn't hurt to speak.

He pulled himself into a sitting position, and looked to the spot where Khaine had fallen. His mentor had vanished, consumed by the pure manna from Elisa's sword and her will. Her blade lay on the cold stone floor, glowing a dull, angry crimson with purpose.

His words, though, echoed in D'Arden's mind.

You, who have only been introduced to the manna within the last few days, have a greater potential than any who have been suppressed by the heartblade...

A cold shudder went through him as Elisa helped him to his feet.

"I think we won," she said softly.

D'Arden stared at her. The natural green of her eyes was completely overtaken by the shining, burning blue of the manna that radiated outward from her. It was almost eerie looking at her, the newest of his Order... and wondering at what unimaginable potential lay behind those eyes.

"I think you're right," he answered after a moment.

**

Once they had recovered enough to walk, they left the dusty fortress behind them. D'Arden could feel the sudden clarity in the air; the dark swirls of corruption surrounding the fortress had vanished into the void along with Khaine. Even the sun itself seemed to be warmer upon the land. Calessa was still desolate, its streets empty of life, but now people could return to this place.

The sudden clarity alerted D'Arden's attention to one thing. As his ability to read the flows of manna came to him again, as the fog of corruption lifted, his mind was drawn to a certain place.

There was still evil in Calessa.

He left Elisa to gather the horse from the stable at the inn, and gave her enough coin to purchase a temporary steed for herself. She would be given an acolyte's horse once they reached the Tower, but his destrier would not be strong enough to carry them the whole way.

Once she was well on to her task, D'Arden told her that he would return shortly. She was not yet experienced enough to read the flows of manna as he was, so she was blissfully unaware of the evil that still remained here. It was not strong, but D'Arden could sense from where it came from in the clarity of the streams even without nearing a manna font.

He had found his demon.

D'Arden was still at only a fraction of his strength,

but he had no choice. He had been sent to cleanse the evil from Calessa, and he had every intention of completing his task.

Up the steps and into the soldier's barracks he went, brushing past the young soldiers standing there without a word. He had wondered why none of these soldiers were older, why so many of them were so young. It hadn't dawned on him then, but now he knew.

D'Arden strode up to the door of the captain's chamber and rapped sharply on the door. A voice came from within, bade him enter. He opened the door and stepped inside.

Captain Mor greeted him with a broad smile. "So, Arbiter. You've cleansed Calessa of its evil. It must be a great thing, to know that you have achieved such wonders in your short time here, and succeeded where your predecessor did not."

"You made many mistakes, demon," D'Arden said calmly. "Many of them I did not recognize when I should have. It is true that I have cleansed Calessa of the corruption, but I have not removed all of the evil from within its walls. Despite what you told me previously, I know that it was you who drove Havox Khaine into the labyrinth beneath the old fortress, who told him of the corruption there. I know it was you who drove him mad beneath that awful place, and turned him into your own avatar of corruption."

"So, you found me out," Mor sighed. "I should have expected that this moment would come. Know this, though, before you snuff out my light, Arbiter. Your friend Khaine was mad from the moment he walked through our gates. Something had touched him long before he ever came within my domain. I saw in him a chance to create something great, and so I did. I never expected that there would be someone who would best him. I certainly never expected to be found out by one of your ilk."

"I don't believe you," D'Arden said. "I knew Havox Khaine. He would never have turned into something like that on his own."

"Believe what you like," the guard captain – the demon – said with a shrug. "Is it my fault that you cannot realize that even demons can occasionally speak the truth?"

The Arbiter paused. He and Khaine had once battled a demon on a great mountain, who had put up a terrible fight for many days, before simply standing aside and allowing Khaine to destroy it. After that, Khaine had been recalled to the Tower, while D'Arden was sent alone on his journeyman expedition.

Could that have been where it began to go wrong?

"Sometimes, a simple choice – whether or not to destroy an unarmed opponent, regardless of that opponent's heritage – can be the beginning of the road to madness," the demon said quietly.

D'Arden could stand no more. He drew his blade and swung it outward, cutting through the unmoving neck of the demon with one stroke. The azure flames burst into brilliant light and consumed the deep corruption of the demon's body in mere seconds. It did not fight back; it did not attempt to flee, but simply accepted its fate.

Just like the demon on the mountain.

The Arbiter stared as the last flickers of azure light vanished, and a soul-deep chill ran down his spine.

As he walked from the room, he turned to the first soldier that he found, who happened to be the young man who'd greeted him at Calessa's gate. He sized up the young soldier in a moment – there was no trace of corruption or evil within him. The soldier stared back into his eyes confidently, though there was a small amount of surprise within them.

"What's your name, soldier?" D'Arden asked him.

"Mayer, sir," the young man responded.

"By the order of the Arbiter's Tower, you are hereby promoted to the rank of Guard Captain of Calessa, Liaison to the Tower. Captain Mor has been found guilty of succumbing to corruption and seeking to destroy the city, and has been summarily executed. Aid will be coming in the next few weeks directly from the Tower to assist you in cleansing Calessa Heights and to help with rebuilding efforts." D'Arden rattled this off as quickly as possible so as not to give the soldier a chance to argue or ask questions. "You will be responsible for coordinating the aid along with the citizenry. Is this understood?"

The young soldier nodded. "Of course, Master Arbiter. I live to serve. But if I may ask…?"

"What is it?" D'Arden asked.

"Exactly what did Captain Mor do, sir? He was the best Guard Captain that Calessa had seen in a decade."

D'Arden considered lying to the soldier, to tell him that Mor had been a good man who'd simply been overwhelmed by the power of evil. Instead, though, he elected to simply tell the truth in this circumstance. "Captain Mor was a disguised demon."

Mayer's jaw dropped. "Really?"

"Unfortunately," D'Arden said. "I liked the man, too."

"So did I, sir."

"You understand the duties that I now require of you?" D'Arden asked him.

He nodded sharply. "Yes, sir."

"Good, then," D'Arden said. "I leave the city in your hands… Captain Mayer."

**

The sun was setting over the western horizon when D'Arden retrieved Elisa from the stables. His great destrier, Tyral, seemed unusually happy to have her aboard, and had nipped at D'Arden's hand when he tried to take his own saddle back. With amusement, D'Arden had purchased a second horse for him to ride on their way back, since Tyral was so taken with the girl.

Elisa had changed into some of his spare clothing – a breach of protocol, but a necessity, since they had no time for fitting and her fine white tunic was crusted so heavily with blood that it was a total loss. As they mounted their steeds and began to ride towards the gate, D'Arden cast a glance backwards at the inn that stood in the trade square.

In the doorway stood the strange innkeeper, who gave a half-wave and a crooked smile in his direction.

Now, travel almost five thousand years into the history of the world called Eisengoth, to the moment when the first blow was struck in a war that would last for generations; a war that would change the face of the world irrevocably.

An exclusive short story available only in this print edition, the age of darkness begins here...

ON THE LAST DAY OF LIGHT

"This assignment is pointless," Ketan grumbled.

"Patience, Ketan," Master Valira said, raising one hand to placate the youth. "It is true that the Lords of the Nine can be difficult, but we must have patience. King Gandram is a blustery old man without a doubt, but even he will come to see the wisdom of this treaty."

Ketan opened his mouth to speak further, but a sharp glance from Valira silenced him. Instead, he huffed out a sigh.

Valira chuckled. Her apprentice was young and headstrong. The boy was less than half her fifty years; she was old enough to be his grandmother. Fresh blood kept the order from stagnating, it was true, but Valira barely remembered being his age. Diplomacy was always the most difficult on the young, she knew. They preferred action to words, violence to politics. If the world were ruled by those with as few years as Ketan, it would be a sad and dangerous world indeed.

King Gandram was loud, obnoxious, fat and boisterous; there was no doubt about any of these things. He was already beginning to come around, though, which Valira knew that he would inevitably do. She was a Warden, declared to neutrality, a diplomat and defender of right and justice in the Nine Kingdoms, and a devoted servant of the Goddess. To refuse a Warden hospitality was to abandon all hope of maintaining respect in the realm of politics, and to deny a Warden a fair hearing was to bring down the scorn of all the Nine upon one's head.

If there was no chance that Gandram would eventually side with the treaty, the Conclave would never have sent her all the way out to the very edges of the Kingdoms. Despite his loud objections, intelligence must have suggested that his opinion was malleable, and she had seen much the same in their negotiations. Before she left, King Gandram would not only sign the treaty, but he would do it gladly.

She planned to make sure of it.

Gandram was meeting with his advisors overnight, and as per the Accords, the King was required to provide them with accommodations. They were housed in the east wing of his rather humble estate, in a large guest suite on the second floor. The bed was opulent and entirely unnecessary, as a Warden's discipline training encouraged her to sleep in only a simple bedroll, no matter what minor aches and pains might be coming on as a result of her age. Sharing the room with her apprentice was no more an inconvenience; in fact, it allowed her to keep an eye on him.

Ketan stalked over to the doors that led out to the balcony, threw them open wide, and looked out. From her position in the room, Valira could see past his shoulder and out over the balustrade. The warm white light of the Goddess' Eye shone down, bathing the rolling green hills in soft gray tones. It was a marvelous sight, and it filled her heart with joy.

He looked up at the sky, and Valira watched a strange expression creep over her apprentice's face. "Master... what...?"

"What is it, Ketan?" she asked.

"I'm... I'm not sure," he answered, his eyes fixated upward.

She rose from her seat and crossed to the window,

standing beside Ketan, and cast her gaze to the sky.

At the edge of the pale golden disk was what appeared to be a stain from some kind of red liquid. As she watched, it slowly grew into a ragged red line, looking for all the world like a bloody gash across the face of the moon.

What she was seeing was impossible.

Then, before her eyes, the entire moon turned bright red.

All around her, the land which had seemed so peaceful in the warm yellow light suddenly seemed dark and foreboding. Instead of soft grays and whites, everything was an ugly brown or stark blood red. Her breath caught in her throat, and her head swam with the sheer wrongness of it all.

"What's happening?" Ketan whispered, incredulous.

"I don't know," Valira said.

In that moment, the screaming began.

A sound like ripping cloth came from the room behind her, though it was as loud as a crack of thunder. She whirled to see a ragged red gash open in the very air of the stateroom, and a malevolent red light poured through it.

As she watched, a creature stepped through the tear; a creature made of nightmares. It was bulbous and misshapen, so asymmetric it hurt the eyes to look upon it. Uncountable legs skittered across the floor and a writhing cluster of dark tentacles reached out from the thing's central mass. It made a kind of chittering sound as it launched itself across the stone floor at her, rushing at a speed that seemed impossible.

"Ketan - get down!" she cried, diving across the floor to avoid the bull rush. Her apprentice flung himself in the opposite direction, but the creature pursued him, changing its course almost effortlessly. Ketan let out a cry of fear and anguish as the thing bore down on him.

Valira rolled to a crouch and flung out her hand. "Kettek!" she cried.

White light formed around her hand in the blink of an eye, and leapt away from her fingers as though fired from a crossbow. The creature leapt into the air as it pounced toward Ketan, but the burst of magical fire caught it somewhere near the center of mass and flung it off its trajectory. The thing flew over Ketan's prone form and slammed into the wall on the far side of the room.

"Get your sword, Ketan!" Valira shouted, sprinting for the wardrobe where she had placed her blade.

She reached the doors of the wardrobe and reached out her hand to open them. As she did, the weight of the creature crashed into her from the side, throwing them both to the floor. Valira cried out and rolled, using the momentum and the strength of her legs to catch the thing in its midsection and fling it off of her. The hairy legs of the creature and the reaching tentacles scrabbled at her, but found no purchase, as she shoved it into the air away from her.

Valira knew that she had only seconds. She sprang to her feet and made it to the wardrobe, flinging its doors open so hard that they careened off the walls on either side. She grabbed the thin leather scabbard with her left hand and the hilt of her sword with the right and spun. As she turned, she pulled the sword free to cut through the air behind her, feeling that the creature was upon her.

White light flared as the crystalline sword came free from its sheath, slashing a glowing arc through the creature

iv

as it leapt at her. The razor-sharp edge cut straight through the thing - legs, tentacles and body mass together. It let out a scream from some unknown orifice as its pounce was interrupted and the sword bisected it. The two halves of the thing tumbled to either side and vanished in a swirl of dark red smoke, leaving behind only a foul stench.

She stood there for a moment, panting from the exertion, the white light from her crystal sword illuminating her in the darkened chamber. All of the candles and lanterns had sputtered out. The only remaining light was from the blade of her sword, and from a dull, shimmering crimson glow from that ragged slash which hung in the air only a few feet away from her.

"What was that thing?" Ketan asked, coming to her side.

She glanced at him, and her mouth formed into a hard line. "Where is your sword, apprentice?" she snapped.

His eyes glanced to hers and then away, guiltily. It took him only seconds to retrieve his sword from where he had placed it near the door. Pure ivory light shone forth as he drew his own crystalline sword from its sheath.

"To answer your question," she said, once his sword was drawn, "I have no idea what that was... or what that is." She gestured to the shimmering hole in the air with her scabbard. "Whatever it is, I do not believe we have seen the last of those things."

He gaped at her. "You think there are more?"

She cocked her head. The screaming was not her imagination - it was coming from all over the castle, audible even through the stone walls, and it had not abated. "Something is very wrong, Ketan. We must flee this place immediately and return to the Conclave."

"What about the people here?" he asked.

"You and I cannot stand alone against an army of those creatures," she said. "If we are to have any hope of helping anyone, we must get to the drakes and fly straight for the Conclave. If this is not happening everywhere in the Nine Kingdoms - and I pray to the Goddess that it is not - we may have a chance of mobilizing enough Wardens and Magi to stop this strange invasion before it gets worse."

"And if it is happening everywhere?" he asked.

She looked at him with a deep sorrow in her eyes. "Then I fear all may be lost."

Valira turned to the ragged gash in the air - it was a gate, she realized, a passage from some other place or time - and lifted one hand toward it. She reached out with the magic she possessed and probed it gently, trying to determine more about it without triggering it or disturbing it somehow. The feelings it radiated made her stomach twist, and bile rose in her throat. It was disgusting, horrifying, wrong somehow, as though reality itself were wounded.

It would not heal, no matter how lightly she touched. Every drop of power she directed toward the gate seemed to be sucked in and vanished beyond it. The feeling of sickness grew worse as she examined it, and then there was a pulse of agony that went through her head.

Another of those creatures was about to come through.

Steeling her will, she began to rapidly assemble a cage of magical energy around it. With her hands and her mind she worked the power in the air, whispering words in a spidery tongue under her breath as she placed each invisible keystone. Mere seconds after she laid the last point and muttered the invocation under her breath, another of the nightmare creatures emerged through. It slammed up against the wall of the magical prison, and let out a shriek that nearly caused her ears to bleed.

"That won't hold them forever," she gasped, exhausted from the effort. "Come, Ketan. We must go."

She made sure that the doors closed securely behind them as they left the room. Valira made her way swiftly along the long stone corridor, with Ketan close at her heels. The only light was the blood red glow of the moon filtering through the slits in the walls, and the pale illumination from their swords.

The metallic stench of blood hung in the air, and screams reverberated off the walls, though there were fewer of those now. It made Valira sick to think about how many voices had been silenced at the hands of those creatures.

She turned a corner that would lead them to the great staircase leading down to the main hall of the castle, from which they could make their escape to the drake roost. As her eyes surveyed the scene before her, she heard Ketan clap one hand over his mouth and fight the urge to be sick. Her own stomach turned.

Another of those strange gates pulsed angrily in the air near the center of the hall. Around it was a scene that could have come straight out of an abbatoir. Dismembered corpses covered the floor, were pushed up against the walls, and the stone had turned bright red with the spilled blood. The smell of iron mixed with offal here, and she steeled herself against the vision of carnage before her. White bone was clearly visible in too many places; milky, staring eyes wide with horror gaped in every direction.

Behind her, Ketan spilled the meager contents of his stomach on the floor. It took everything she had to keep from doing the same. She was a diplomat, for the Goddess' sake. While it was true that every Warden was trained as a warrior, she rarely had to use those skills. Reputation and persuasion were the hallmarks of the Conclave, not death and violence.

"Their spirits reside with the Goddess now," she said, exerting iron control over her voice to keep it from breaking. "We must leave them to their rest."

Ketan nodded weakly, and followed as she strode boldly across the blood-soaked carpet, trying to ignore the squelching sound her boots made as she did. It was by no means an easy thing to do, but somehow she managed it.

The next corner revealed the great staircase, which wound down through the air and into the main hall below. Shrieks of pain and agony rose up from the floor below, and Valira tried to close her ears against the sound. We must escape, and warn the Conclave...

"Hurry, Ketan," she said over her shoulder. "If we make all haste, we should be able to reach the drake roost in short order."

"Of course, Master," he said, but she could hear the illness and trepidation in his voice. He did not have the years of diplomatic training which had taught her to conceal every emotion as she spoke, lest her bargaining position give her away. He might never get it, now. It seemed that the world was about to need warriors far more than it needed diplomats.

They raced down the stairs, leaving footprints of blood in their wake. Valira was the first to set foot on the landing, and the horrors she saw before her would have broken a lesser mind. As her eyes swept around the grisly scene before her, she considered simply collapsing to the ground and breaking down in shuddering sobs.

The great foyer was full of those skittering creatures. Servants and other residents of the King's manor lay scattered in every direction like a child's discarded toys. Some of them, she realized with horror, were still alive. Weak moans and the occasional shriek filled the air as the creatures devoured them, dismembered them, tore them apart with no regard for suffering. These were not predators; they were not interested solely in food. These creatures existed to maximize suffering.

As she stood there, stunned at the depths of depravity around her, she slowly realized that the creatures were turning their attention to her and Ketan - away from their helpless meals. One by one, the tentacled masses stopped what they were doing and turned to her, clicking their legs and writhing their appendages in anticipation.

She lowered herself into a combat crouch, gripping her crystal sword so tightly that her knuckles were white around the hilt. A dull ache throbbed in her knee, and in that moment she became keenly aware of her age. There was no way she could fight all of them off.

In the floor beneath her feet there came a tremor, and then another. Thunder split the air, and a massive ragged gate opened before her very eyes. As the fabric of reality tore asunder, Valira was certain that she could hear the echoing screams of the damned issue forth from that horrific fissure.

What stepped through the gate was so monstrous, so grotesque that even the skittering horrors cowered in awe. A misshapen, bipedal creature that appeared to be some twisted mockery of a human being passed through the tear between realities - bow-legged and awkward, yet moving with a preternatural grace that made her head swim. Three monstrous arms, one on each side and one reaching up from behind it like a scorpion's tail, each ended in two bulbous fingers, from which protruded claws as long as her arm that glowed a deep scarlet. There was no head to speak of, but two flickering candle-flames of that same crimson light floated in mid-air above its huge, ungainly chest, approximately where the head of the creature should have been. A red mist poured off the creature, as though it were shedding aspirated blood from every part of it.

Valira's breath caught in her throat. Though she had never before laid eyes on such a monstrosity, she recognized those eyes, like twin candles burning in the air with no fuel and a deep, unknowable malevolence. She had seen representations of them in the oldest books kept by the Conclave, relics of an age which was all but forgotten to the world, remembered only in writing, and stories told to horrify children and keep them from staying out too late in the dark.

"Old One," she breathed. "The Banished."

Those hovering eyes fixated on her as the Old One turned its bulk toward her. She felt the blood rush to her ears and her vision darkened at the edges, pulsing in time with her rising heartbeat. The creature's scrutiny, its attention, was almost more than her mind could bear. Screams and cries from beyond the boundaries of the world itself rang in her ears.

SO, the Old One said, though it did not so much speak as project the thoughts directly into her mind. THERE ARE THOSE WHO REMEMBER US.

She felt her hands trembling, but she forced herself to raise the white glow of her sword between her and the Old One. "The Goddess banished you," she whispered. "She sent you away forever. You were never to return to this world again."

A deep, horrible sound pierced through her mind, causing her to cry out and shut her eyes against it, though it did nothing to stop it. Only after a moment did she realize that the Old One was laughing at her.

LONG HAVE WE AWAITED THIS DAY, it laughed. SOON YOUR GODDESS WILL DIE, AND HER CREATION WILL FALL SOON AFTER. YOU ARE WEAK, CODDLED CREATURES. YOU CANNOT STAND AGAINST OUR ARMIES.

"She can never die," Valira said. "She is eternal."

The Old One took a step forward. YOU ARE WRONG.

From behind her, Valira heard the doors to the foyer crash inward, followed by the war cries of more than a dozen men.

"Warden!" cried the voice of the fat King Gandram. "To us!"

"Stay back, Your Highness!" Valira called out. "This creature is far too dangerous for your men!"

"My guardsmen are the finest in all of the Nine!" Gandram shouted back. "To arms, men! Rend the beast limb from limb!"

Screaming cries of war and various profanities in various languages, the King and his eight remaining guards, all heavily armed head-to-toe in thick steel armor and wielding bright steel swords, charged toward the Old One. Valira shot only one glance at them over her shoulder, and saw the skittering beasts getting ready to pounce - but out of the corner of her eye, she saw the Old One make a sort of gesture with its claws, and they waited.

They waited.

The sound of laughter came again, cutting through her mind and threatening to separate her sanity from the rest of her. She clutched her head in agony, nearly collapsing to the ground, but Ketan caught her and kept her up.

"Master... are you all right?" the boy asked.

It was that moment that Valira realized that the laughter was intended only for her.

"Your Highness, please - stop! Run, do not fight this creature!" she shouted over the Old One's mocking laugh.

King Gandram paid her no heed.

As the eight armored warriors - and one very fat King - closed with the Old One, it struck out with its claws, faster than a flash of lightning. The crimson scythes at the end of the Old One's hands sliced through steel as though it were paper, severing swords and burning through armor, flesh and bone in a single stroke. The war cries were choked off, immediately replaced with screams of pain and terror. The few lucky strokes that made it past the Old One's preternatural defenses simply careened off its bulbous hide as though they had struck a stone wall.

With two more strokes of its claws, the Old One killed the last of the guards, leaving them nothing but ruined, bloody and charred wrecks in a circle around it.

Then, it turned its fiery eyes back to her.

NOW DO YOU SEE? it asked as its gaze bore into her. DO YOU UNDERSTAND?

"The Goddess will defeat you," she gasped, leaning

heavily on Ketan.

"Is... is that thing talking to you?" her apprentice asked, his voice a whisper in her ear.

YOU STILL DO NOT UNDERSTAND MY POWER, the Old One said, its tone almost... disappointed, somehow. VERY WELL THEN. I SHALL DEMONSTRATE.

COME TO ME.

A jolt went through Valira as the command wracked her body, but it was not intended for her. Ketan stiffened, and then his arms went limp. She fell to her knees on the blood-soaked floor, barely managing to hold onto her sword, as her apprentice stopped supporting her weight. She cried out, nearly blinded by the agony in her head.

Through a haze of pain and fear, she watched as Ketan moved in short, jerky motions, like a puppet controlled by an amateur. He placed one foot ahead of the next, walking slowly toward the Old One.

"Master..." he said, his voice breaking. "H... help me..."

Valira tried to surge to her feet, but she was blasted back to her knees by a wave of pain that threatened to rob her of consciousness.

YOU WILL LEARN.

"P... please, Master Valira!" Ketan cried. "I... I can't stop..."

"Don't hurt him!" Valira shouted. "He's just a boy!"

Ketan took another step forward, and then another. He began to sob; thick, choking sounds coming from his throat as his hand went limp and his crystal sword dropped to the ground. The white light sputtered and went dark.

Valira tried again to rise, but the Old One's power

held her fast. If she tried to move at all, pain so intense that it literally blinded her flashed through the center of her being. She closed her eyes and bowed her head.

"I'm sorry, Ketan," she whispered, tears running down her face.

LOOK AT ME, the Old One commanded, and her head jerked up, her eyes forced open by some invisible force.

Ketan now stood only inches away from the Old One. He gasped cries of terror between the sobs. The fiery eyes turned downward to regard the boy.

Tears blurred Valira's vision as the screams began, for which she could not help but be thankful. Through the salty wetness in her eyes, she watched as the Old One skinned her apprentice alive.

When Ketan's screams finally choked off and went silent, the power holding her in place released her, and she tumbled face-first to the bloodied floor. She lay there for what seemed like an eternity, knowing that her turn was next.

It never came.

Finding reserves of strength she never knew existed, Valira managed to get her hands on the floor and pushed herself up.

The Old One and all of the skittering beasts were gone.

The doors that led to the courtyard outside were smashed to pieces. She did not recall hearing the creatures destroy it. Outside, the land was bathed in red much as the interior of the castle was, the light of the bloody moon casting everything in a malevolent glow.

She had dropped her sword, its light had gone. When

she picked it back up, the ivory light flickered, but did not ignite. It sputtered like a candle flame in a breeze, never quite springing back to the life the way it should have.

Valira staggered forward, through the shattered doors and into the light of the red moon. She cast her gaze around the courtyard, struggling to stay focused, feeling as though she were on the edge of a vast precipice. Whispers sounded at the edges of her hearing, too quiet to make out but too loud to be mistakeable - yet there was no one alive in sight.

Her eyes fell on the center of the courtyard, where a circle of white stones had marked a central gathering place. In long, charred marks across the stone, a message was spelled out in harsh, jagged strokes.

RUN. TELL THEM. WARN THEM. YOU WILL PREPARE, YOU WILL FIGHT, AND THEN YOU WILL DIE.

THIS IS THE WAY OF THINGS.

Beneath the bloodied eye of her goddess, Valira fell to her knees and wept.

****

So ends the first strike in the conflict which would come to be known as the Godswar, when the legions of forgotten dark deities invaded the world of Eisengoth and took up arms against its loyal defenders; the war which gave rise to the deadly defenders of purity known as the Arbiters...

Afterword

ELEGY is but the first step in the tale of D'Arden Tal and his apprentice, Elisa. LEGACY: Book 2 of the Arbiter Codex is forthcoming, exploring the greatest disaster to befall the Arbiters in millennia, and the currently-untitled third book will follow.

If you enjoyed ELEGY, you may also enjoy my two novelettes, currently available in ebook format: THE CORPSE KING and SORCERER'S CODE. Find them on the Amazon Kindle store or Smashwords.com!

For more information on my work and the world of Eisengoth, visit my website at:

http://www.christopherkellen.com

The Corpse King

After years of nothing but grueling training and the desperate dance of death that is the life of an acolyte Arbiter, D'Arden Tal has been named an apprentice. He has been assigned to learn from Havox Khaine, one of the greatest Masters in living memory.

For two years they have traveled across the known world, and now they enter a tiny kingdom on the edge of nowhere. Rumors abound that the monarch of this kingdom is insane, and has created a demented puppet court... of the dead.

D'Arden must learn what it truly means to be an Arbiter, as he makes his first real confrontation with the horrors of corruption. Something much worse lurks within the shadows of the king's mind than simple madness, and D'Arden will find reason to call him...

The Corpse King.

Find out more at
http://www.christopherkellen.com/

Sorcerer's Code

Edar Moncrief: sorcerer and scholar extraordinaire. To the outside world, he is a peddler of love potions and wart remover – after all, one has to make a living. Behind closed doors, he is a dangerous and powerful sorcerer specializing in the laws and function of the mysterious energy known as manna.

When he trips over a body in the streets of Elenia, he discovers that the corpse belongs to none other than an Arbiter, the mysterious wielders of the crystal swords rarely seen in his part of the world. The loss of life is his gain, though, when he finds the opportunity to examine the most precious and rare artifact in the world: the Arbiter's heartblade.

To his misfortune, that same opportunity brings him face-to-face with the spectre of death. Another Arbiter, D'Arden Tal, has found him, and believes he is responsible for the killing. Edar's only hope is to find and catch a murderer in the streets of the most decadent and deadly city in the Old Kingdoms, before Tal declares him responsible and kills him instead…

Find out more at
http://www.christopherkellen.com/

ABOUT THE AUTHOR

Christopher Kellen is an IT specialist who thinks he's got what it takes to spin the occasional swords-and-sorcery yarn. His heroes of literature are those who are fearless in telling an uncompromising story. He wishes that there were more people who wrote like Robert E. Howard, H.P. Lovecraft, and Karl Edward Wagner, and while he knows that that he can never live up to their genius, he hopes to contribute something to the genre that they so loved. He lives in New Hampshire with his wife and their monstrous black dog.